JUSTICE FOR ANIMALS
TEXAS STYLE

Cynthia Herschkowitsch

JUSTICE for ANIMALS: Texas Style
© Cynthia Herschkowitsch, 2016

Book and cover design by Jeanne Ann Macejko.

Other books by Cynthia Herschkowitsch
Ling-Ling's Story
Oma: A Heroine of the Holocaust

CreateSpace Independent Publishing Platform
North Charleston, S.C.

For additional information, contact:
Cynthia Herschkowitsch
Hersch48@peoplepc.com

Acknowledgements

First and foremost, I must thank my cohorts in the Farmers Branch Writers' Organization for their support, advice and encouragement throughout the writing process. A special thanks goes to my mentors, Jeanne Macejko and Carol A. Caldwell, whose input has been priceless. Jeanne has been instrumental in helping me, a fledgling author, accomplish my goals of publishing two non-fiction books: *Ling Ling's Story* and *Oma: A Heroine of the Holocaust* and, now this work of fiction. Thanks to the Manske Library in Farmers Branch, Texas, for supporting the local writers' group.

I also want to thank my students who served as inspiration for Frau's comrades in the story and especially to my dear friend and colleague Ray Hernandez who served as a model for my fictional detective. Gerardo Ramos deserves a lot of credit for lending his technical expertise and suggesting plot twists. My family deserves my gratitude for encouraging my writing endeavors, reading my early drafts and helping with editing.

Most of all, I must acknowledge the many pets that I have loved and protected throughout my life who inspired this story. If everyone loved animals as much as I do, there would be no revenge story to write. Virtually every time that I read the newspaper or watch television, there is a story of horrific abuse, locally and internationally. From people who abuse their own pets in secret to the people who kill endangered animals as trophies, it makes sickening news. I commend the many people who are on the front lines, working to protect animals and bring their suffering to light. There is a contingent of people in Dallas alone who work tirelessly to save animals from abuse or seek justice for those who did not survive. I can't adequately convey my heartfelt gratitude for the many people who go to city shelters to save animals, like my friend Tawanna Couch, who literally pulls animals from death row and flies them up north where they are adopted by loving families. My friend Jonnie England sits in on every trial of every animal abuser to let the perpetrator know that there are people who care and to seek justice for the animal victims. She and Skip Trimble, among others, have fought to persuade legislators to pass bills to protect animals and prosecute offenders. Angie Manriquez, the "fairy dogmother of West Dallas" and Marina Tarashevska, the angel of Dowdy Ferry Road, spend their time and money to help animal victims and, if nothing else, to give them respect in death. Let us all be mindful of the fact that every animal deserves to live with a family who will love and protect them, cherish and care for them until their dying day.

1

No one knew what made Frau Geiger snap. Some galvanizing incident forever changed her life, but she wasn't telling. At first, the effect wasn't obvious, but as she grew older, it weighed heavier on her mind. And she knew, sooner or later, that she would act on it. With a vengeance.

It first surfaced when, after many years of teaching high school, one of her students casually observed, "Frau, you can't ever retire. You know you would miss us and, besides, what would you do?" He seemed awfully sure of himself.

She looked at him for a moment and, just as casually, said, "I'm going to retire so I can be an assassin."

The whole class looked up, shocked. No one said anything. Finally, a nervous voice ventured, "Who are you going to assassinate, Frau?"

"I'm going to assassinate those guys that kill the baby seals."

"Oh, come on, Frau," Victor said. "You can't even kill ants and roaches in the classroom. And remember how you and Trebor, and Ebony, and I peeled that baby mouse's tiny toes off that glue board one at a time? You don't have it in you to kill."

"Nevertheless, that's my plan. If you think about it, I would make the perfect assassin. A little old retired school teacher? Who would suspect me? Now, Jose, over there, that's another matter. When you look at him, you immediately suspect he's up to no good."

Jose laughed in agreement.

"I, on the other hand, look completely innocent. I will blend right in, wherever I need to go. 'Frau, come right in,' they will say. And I will walk in with a whole arsenal. You know I have a concealed handgun license. I'm preparing for this."

Everyone laughed. The thought of tiny Frau Geiger as an assassin was hilarious. Some members of her award-winning academic team had known her for years. Because of their bond, forged during three years of intense preparation and competitions, Valentine fund-raisers for the SPCA and Christmas parties for needy children, they knew she probably wasn't kidding. Given the chance, she would annihilate anyone who hurt an animal. She frequently rescued stray animals that wandered onto the school campus, often enlisting the students' help. More than once, they had taken turns during class bottle-feeding tiny puppies whose mothers had been hit by a car or just disappeared. At the end of the day, she would manage to find fosters for them or convince rescue groups to take them in. They knew about her soft spot for animals, so it made sense that she would champion baby seals with those big, trusting, luminous eyes.

At the back of the room, Gino nodded in polite agreement with the others. But as always, he was skeptical. He liked Frau Geiger. He thought she was a little crazy at times, but he admired her dedication and perseverance. He also liked the idea of a woman who would take action and stand up for her beliefs. He sighed. *A woman like Scarlett Johansen. That's what I need. She can really kick ass!* Scarlett was his dream woman, the star of the movies that replayed in his head. He would be the director; she would be his star. Although he was headed to a Texas university to major in engineering, he really wanted to direct movies. Action movies with lots of cool toys, violent explosions, and mayhem. He shook himself out of his reverie to hear Frau Geiger say, "For the next class, read the articles about Maria Theresa and the social/political factors leading up to the French Revolution."

Jackson was equally skeptical. He had just enrolled this year and had not known Frau Geiger as long as the others had. But he knew her by reputation, because she had taught his older brothers and sisters. He knew her passions for teaching and animals. As soon as he enrolled, he told his counselor, "I want to be in Ms. Geiger's class."

"Unfortunately," she told him, "That's a special class by teacher invitation only, so unless you get her approval, I can't put it on your schedule."

Just then, as if on cue, Frau Geiger walked through the counselor's suite, looked directly at him, and asked, "Are you one of those West kids?"

His smile was her answer. The West kids had very strong genes; tall, good-looking, brown-skinned kids with huge smiles, featuring perfectly aligned, impossibly white teeth, they stood out in any crowd.

"Why, yes, I am. And you must be Ms. Geiger," he answered. "Gwendolyn and Georgia told me I have to take your class." Georgia had been the Valedictorian of her class. In addition to being good-looking, the West kids were incredibly smart.

"It's done!" she said and turned to his counselor: "Jennifer, please see if Mr. West has room in his schedule for the academic team."

And that's how Frau came to know Jackson West. Besides his sterling lineage, Jackson had one attribute that led to immediate fame at the school and had people referring to him as "The Voice." Smooth, mellifluous, and sophisticated, it was the voice of a much older, dignified gentleman, honed from years of speaking at his church. Accomplished as a speaker at such an early age, Jackson was just sixteen when he made his presentation for the church elders in Atlanta and was ordained a youth minister.

As soon as their principal—a bit of a stutterer himself—heard Jackson speak, he said, "I want that guy doing announcements!"

Soon, everyone knew him. His first day on the public address system, he seemed like such an old pro that everyone was looking around and asking, "Who is that guy?" They assumed it was a new teacher, but word soon got around that it was the new student, the one who went to Greenhill and Richardson and was home-schooled. Everyone wanted to meet him. Girls wanted to hug him; boys wanted to shake his hand. He was reeking with charisma but was humbly unaware of it.

Frau Geiger knew she wanted these two on her team.

2

When they graduated, Jackson earned the distinction of being selected "Mr. Senior" by his classmates, while Gino emerged as Valedictorian in a surprise, come-from-behind takeover. For years, he had been number three in the class and was resigned to it. However, the student who was number one made a tragic mistake by dropping an Advanced Placement class in her final semester. With his determination and unflagging work ethic, Gino never strayed off-course and easily leaped over the number two girl to capture the number one spot. That secured him the scholarship he wanted. Although he toyed with the idea of going to MIT, he eventually settled on UT Austin, which was just far enough away to exercise some independence, but not so far that it would preclude the occasional trip home.

During the three years in Frau's class, Gino had become more outgoing. He often confided in her and sought her advice. It was clear that he had reservations about going away to school; it was also clear that he needed to get away from his family.

Frau told him, "Gino, the first two weeks will be the hardest. You're going to be homesick, for sure."

"Well, I don't know about that," he said. "It will be good to get away from my mom. She asks too many questions and wants to get in my business all the time."

"Oh, Gino, your mother was always the first one to bring you to contests and events. She seems very devoted."

"That's what she would like you to think," he coolly observed. "Anything else?"

"Well, if you get lonely those first two weeks, just call me. I'll talk you through it. By the end of your first month, you'll probably have met some people. Just get involved. Join a study group. Establish a routine. That always helps."

"Got it," he replied. "I'll be back to help you with the Christmas party."

On the other hand, Jackson left for a prestigious university on the west coast and never looked back. Completely self-assured from his years of public speaking, he had no regrets about being so far from home. Besides, he had relatives and church friends in California; it was like a second home.

At Homecoming in late October, he came back to hand over his "Mr. Senior" crown to his successor, but it was a trade-off with Thanksgiving. He couldn't afford to make both trips, so he spent Thanksgiving with friends on the West Coast. He, too, promised to return for the children's Christmas party which was a big tradition at the school and regularly attended by alumni. For the next four years, both Jackson and Gino were regular fixtures at the event. While they were in town for the holidays, the two made it a point to get together with Frau Geiger for an educational foray, ranging from an ice sculpture exhibit one year at the Gaylord Texan, to the Chihuly glass-blowing exhibit at the Dallas Arboretum, to ice-skating at the Galleria. It was always fun. They would catch-up on school drama, their classmates, world events, plans for the future—whatever captured their imagination. It was then that they began referring to themselves as "Trifecta Perfecta"—the perfect demographic. Frau Geiger, the older "white" female; Gino, a youthful Hispanic male and Jackson, an equally youthful, African-American male. Frau viewed Jackson as the voice of reason, Gino as the tech wiz and herself as the instigator. They still had no idea about the plans she had for them. But, by the third Christmas of their college careers, Gino surprised her with a gift: a black t-shirt with a Ninja cat on it and the caption: "Aww-ssassin."

Hmm, she thought. *I wonder if he's reading my mind?*

After his dismal experience with ice-skating, Gino, who had never skated before, went back to Austin determined to add that to his skill-set. Jackson and Frau had made it look so easy! Although he had a black belt in karate, an activity his father had chosen for him and his siblings, he had never been active in sports, and he wanted to change that. So to his list of (1) learn to swim; (2) learn archery; (3) learn to sky-dive, he added, (4) learn to ice-skate. He didn't think that running with the bulls in Pamplona or diving with sharks was necessarily a sport. They were on his "bucket list," although as Frau reminded him, "At your age, it's a to-do list."

Dutifully, he signed up for ice-skating lessons and attended every Wednesday and Saturday. When the first session ended after six weeks, he felt that his speed still wasn't adequate, so he signed up for another session. At the end of round two, he qualified for the next level, which satisfied his desire to master the sport. For his 22nd birthday, he went sky-diving. Granted, it was tandem, but it was a start. Then he spent a weekend in the spring taking lessons so he could get his motorcycle license, which, Frau wryly noted, wasn't even on his to-do list!

"I know," he told her. "I don't know why I did it. It's not like I have a motorcycle or anything. I just felt somehow that I should get it."

Yeah, she thought. *You're going to need it.*

"Now, how about that swimming? You can't swim with sharks until you know how to, well, swim!" She laughed.

After Gino graduated and moved back to Dallas, he visited often. They had long talks about his future and his increasing confusion over what he should do. Of course, armed with his newly minted degree in mechanical engineering, he applied to a number of companies across the U.S. "But," he confessed to her, "I don't know if that's really what I want to do. I got the degree at my father's urging. And I thought it would be a good idea because I do want to blow-up some stuff."

Perfect, she thought.

"But you know I really would like to go into film directing, and I've also been to the Air Force Recruiting Office. I'm really interested in going in because that's one path to becoming an astronaut." He paused, drumming his fingers on the table. "They want me to lose 35 pounds."

"Well, that's doable," she told him. "It would mean some hard work on your part. But 35 pounds? That's going to leave you really skinny. That's a significant weight loss. What do you weigh now? 175? 180?"

"According to them, it's 165, so I'll be down to, like, 130, but you know you've got to be small to maneuver in a space capsule."

"Like Wolowitz on 'The Big Bang Theory'?" They both laughed at the reference to their favorite television show.

"Yeah," he responded. "I don't want to be that guy."

"Well, you've really got some decisions to make. But I wouldn't mention the astronaut thing to your parents just yet. You know they'll try to talk you out of the military. Make up your mind and then tell them and just do it."

"Yeah, that's the plan."

"In the meantime, I've got some projects I want to run by you. Nothing illegal, but borderline. I wouldn't get you into any career-enders." Frau glanced over her shoulder at him as she retrieved her laptop.

"What are we talking about?" He looked a little nervous.

"Just some payback things. There are evil people out there who need a 'come-to-Jesus meeting.' You know how you told me once that when you hear an ambulance siren, it makes you feel helpless, like you wish you could do something? Well, we're going to do something. Get Jackson and see if he can meet with us at my place."

While Gino texted Jackson, Frau was looking at a map of the Dallas area around Loop 12 and I35. She was fairly familiar with the area, because the high school was nearby, but she wanted to triangulate an event she had read about that morning.

"Okay," Gino said. "Jackson is on his way. You wanna tell me what's up?"

"No, I'll wait for him to get here. It's going to take the collective genius."

Thirty minutes later, Jackson strolled in, nonchalant as usual.

"Hey, Frau, Gino," he nodded in Gino's direction. "What's up?"

"Jackson, I'm convening the Trifecta Perfecta to undertake a little mission. It's payback time."

"What do you mean?" Looking puzzled, he glanced at Gino.

"Okay, here's the deal."

Frau read a letter in the *Dallas Morning News* from an outraged citizen who had seen a man toss two kittens out of his car window in the rush hour traffic. The witness described a silver two-door sedan but did not get a good look at the driver, other than that it seemed to be a brown-skinned man. The location of the incident was on westbound Loop 12, right past the I35 overpass near the Grace Temple Church.

"You know, I used to pass that way every day going home," she said.

Jackson added, "And I've attended many events at that church. So what do you want us to do?"

"Well, I think we need to start at the barber shop."

"Oh, yeah," Jackson agreed. "The Blackvine. If anyone knows anything, it will filter through there."

"Right, so if you go and just ask around, you might pinpoint the creep that did this."

"Yeah, that is, if he's Black. Someone will definitely be bragging."

"That's what I thought, too." Frau bent down to pick up her Siamese cat Charlie, stroking his silky fur as they talked.

"But if he's not Black?"

"Then Gino needs to ask around. What do you think? The paleteros network?"

"Yeah, those ice cream vendors get around. If anybody's talking, they'll know because the kids tell them everything."

"It shouldn't take long to find out who did this heinous thing. And that's when the fun begins." Charlie wriggled free from Frau's grasp and leaped to the floor.

Two days later, they had their answer. The Blackvine yielded no fruit, but the paleteros knew the story: Gustavo Garcia—"Gigi" for short—got mad at his girlfriend for supposedly cheating on him with his cousin. After an angry confrontation, Gigi grabbed her two kittens and jumped in his car, flinging them to their deaths in the early morning traffic. According to the Kidvine, it wasn't the first time he had mistreated animals. He was notorious for using kittens and puppies for bait in training his pit bulls. And he regularly slapped his girlfriend, Perla, around. She stuck with him because she had a baby with him, but word was that her family and friends were encouraging her to dump him and his anger issues before the situation got worse.

Gigi lived over by Kiest Park with his parents and younger sister.

"Okay," Frau began. "We need to do some surveillance. Find out Gigi's schedule, where he works—if he works—when he comes and goes, when he's most likely to be alone."

"I'm on it," Gino said. "I run in that park every evening, so people are used to seeing me. I'll ask around."

"Good deal," Frau said. "I'll go buy the duct tape."

"Duct tape?" They both looked at her in horror.

"Ha-ha. Don't worry," she said. "He won't die. He's just gonna wish he were dead."

Gino and Jackson looked at each other out of the corners of their eyes. This was a side of Frau they'd never seen before.

She sensed their skepticism. "Well, are you in or are you out?"

Gino said, "You know we'll follow you to the ends of the earth, Frau. We just don't want to fall off."

"Relax. I told you it won't end your career or anything. I'll take the fall if it comes to that. I just need your muscle and brains to teach this guy a lesson."

"You never lose that passion for teaching, huh?" Jackson laughed.

"We're going to have to be careful with this. I want to get Gigi in the car of his own volition. I don't want to be charged with kidnapping."

"Let me see first what his routine is," Gino responded. "Maybe he'll need a ride somewhere, and I can simply accommodate him."

On his evening runs in the park—part of his weight loss program—Gino kept his eyes open. He could see Gigi's house on the north side where the trail curved. It appeared that Gigi got home every day around 6:15 PM. Since it was early Fall, it didn't get dark until around 8:00 PM. Gigi was usually gone again by that time. A few discreet inquiries to other park denizens yielded the juicy tidbit that Gigi worked a day job and had a part-time job at the Jack-in-the-Box a few blocks away. Gino communicated the info to Frau.

"Does he work at the Jack's at Illinois and I35?" she asked.

"Yeah. I followed him two times when he left his house. I think he works 8:00 to 1:00 AM, then goes across

35 to that hole-in-the-wall chicken place before he heads home."

"Um, that's interesting. It puts him right where we want him to be, by the highway. But it's a busy intersection. Still . . . it's very doable."

She thought for a few minutes.

"Do you still have that voice-changing gadget that you got when you dressed as Bane for Halloween?"

"Yeah," Gino responded. "It didn't work as well as I wanted, but it was pretty good."

"Okay," she said. "We're gonna need that. And can you come up with a suspension harness of some kind? Something we can strap on a person and lower him with?"

"Where are you going with this, Frau?"

"I think Gigi would benefit from a little fresh air—hanging upside down from the I35 overpass. Serves two purposes: It'll scare the hell out of him and also serve as a warning to anyone else who wants to kill animals. I just hate that. Once you've got the harness ready, we'll run through the plan with Jackson."

A couple of days passed before Gino had his harness ready. *Some leather straps and hooks and a big grappling hook should do the job*, he thought. He tried it out on his uncooperative brother who wanted to know what he was up to. Gino halfway convinced him that he was planning to rappel off a cliff—"Kind of like that guy in Dubai," he told him.

One strap around the waist; one between the legs and two over the shoulders should secure him. Frau said the assemblage had to be quick, so Gino made sure all the buckles worked. He tried it over and over until he could secure the whole apparatus in less than a minute. But, of course, his test dummy was cooperating with him; he doubted Gigi would.

When Frau met again with Jackson and Gino, she had the whole plan mapped out.

When she brought up the voice-changer, Jackson wanted to know why it was necessary.

"Look," Frau said. "I don't want Gigi to be able to tell the cops anything about us. I'll be wearing a red, curly wig and big-framed glasses. I know he's going to guess from my stature that I'm female, but I don't want him to be able to say that you are Black or Hispanic or Anglo, so don't say anything. I'll talk through the voice-changer. If he hears you speak, Jackson, and he tells the cops that you've got a distinctive voice like James Earl Jones or like some Black preacher pounding his pulpit, they'll figure out who you are real quick. Everybody in the 'hood knows your voice. So just let me talk. I'm going to keep it real short."

"Okay, Frau. It's your party. What do you want us to do?" Jackson glanced at Gino skeptically.

As Frau Geiger outlined the plan, Gino and Jackson realized that she had gone a little off the rails. She was right: Gigi was going to wish he were dead.

"Now, just for fun: I came up with an idea that is practical but whimsical. When we're on our little 'adventures,' I'm going to call Gino 'Cobra' and Jackson, 'Viper'."

"Why does Gino get to be Cobra?" Jackson sounded petulant.

"I like it," Gino said, a little self-importantly.

"What's wrong with 'Viper'?" she asked. "They're deadly, fast, and feared throughout the world."

"Well, if you put it that way," he said, sounding somewhat placated.

"But what about you? Which snake are you going to be?"

"What else?" she responded archly. "Black Mamba, baby."

At 11:00 PM, Black Mamba left her home in North Dallas southbound in a silver Corolla that she'd borrowed from a discreet car dealer. Danny was an old friend and loyal. They cleaned out the car, made sure all systems were go, and switched out the license plates for some bogus paper tags. Her choice of cars—designed to look as much as possible like Gigi's silver Corolla, although a slightly newer model—was predicated on her belief that two similar cars would confuse witnesses. She knew how important cars could be in pinpointing criminals. When her neighbor was the victim of a home invasion, a passer-by who knew the homeowner saw a red, older model Plymouth parked in front of the house, backed into the driveway for easy loading and a quick getaway. That car proved to be so distinctive that cops were able to nab the teenage burglars in less than two hours. The pawn receipts were still on the floorboard. Frau knew the necessity of blending in.

At 11:30 PM, she arrived at Cobra's house. He emerged from the sideyard dressed completely in black and tossed his human harness into the back seat.

"Nervous?" she asked.

"Naw, piece of cake." His lie was unconvincing. "Let's roll."

Five minutes later, they picked up Viper, also in black garb.

"What do you want to bet he's been 'flopping'?" Black Mamba directed her question at Cobra, a reference to *A Tale of Two Cities*, when the graverobber told his wife to "quit floppin' against me, woman!" He wanted her to quit praying for him to stop his evildoings.

"Naw, I'm all right, Frau, I mean, Black Mamba."

"Remember, no talking. I know that's hard for you, knowing how you love to hear yourself speak," she teased him.

"Yes, it is difficult. But you weren't wrong about the 'flopping'." Jackson handed Gino a ski mask as he covered his own face.

"Told ya!" Cobra just laughed.

They pulled into a street near the chicken shack and waited, hoping Gigi would not deviate from his routine.

At 1:10 AM, Gigi pulled into the parking lot. Cobra and Viper got out of Frau's car. When Gigi pulled out of the lot, Black Mamba followed him for a block before deliberately rear-ending him.

A very annoyed Gigi got out of his car and approached her window. "My fender is messed up, and I don't have insurance. What are you going to do about this?"

She set the voice-changer to a lower register. "Oh, my foot slipped, and I hit the accelerator instead of the brake." She tried to look apologetic.

As they exchanged unpleasantries, Cobra and Viper approached the cars.

"Look," Black Mamba said. "I don't want this to go on my insurance. We'll work out something. Get in the car and I can write you a check or I'll give you my phone number so you can contact me after you get an estimate."

"All right."

It worked. He got in. In ten seconds, Cobra and Viper jumped into the backseat; Cobra grabbed Gigi from behind.

Black Mamba said, "It will be in your best interest to cooperate."

Terrified, Gigi screamed, "What's this about? Did Victor send you?"

"All in good time, Gigi."

"How do you know my name? What's going on?" Gigi's face was flush with anger and fear.

"Let's take a little drive, and I'll tell you."

"Oh, God," he gasped. "You're not going to kill me, are you? I've got a kid."

"We'll see how it goes. Cobra, are you ready?"

Nodding, Cobra held Gigi in place until Black Mamba stopped the car a half block from the highway overpass.

Viper got the harness ready as Cobra pulled the struggling Gigi from the car. While Cobra held Gigi in a headlock, Viper quickly attached the harness—one strap between the legs, two over the shoulder, one around the waist. He secured them with locks. Gigi struggled, to no avail. Cobra had a death grip on him.

Viper made sure all the straps were secure, and then—the piece de resistance—put duct tape over his mouth. It took less than two minutes to secure him.

"Now, Gigi, would be a good time to start praying," Black Mamba said.

Throwing him into the back seat, they traveled the half block to the overpass. It was 1:30 AM on a Tuesday, the least traveled time on I35 according to statistics.

"Umph. Umph. Umph," Gigi struggled against his restraints, the terror in his eyes a delicious spectacle to Black Mamba.

"What's that you say, Gigi? You peed your pants? Oh, this is nothing. Let's go, team."

Cobra grabbed Gigi while Viper got the cable and began threading it through the harness down to Gigi's feet. Cobra lifted Gigi up over the guard railing and tilted him downward. Viper wrapped the cable around the concrete pillars and secured it with a lock. After insuring that everything was secure, Cobra dropped Gigi, head down, so that he could see oncoming traffic heading right at him. His eyes bulged with horror as headlights beamed in his face.

"Oh, Gigi, you remember how you asked what this is all about? Here it is: Two kittens. That's right. Those two kittens you so callously tossed out the car window. This is the revenge of the kittens! You'd better hope that no eighteen-wheelers come along!" Laughing, the three got in the car, leaving Gigi to dangle from the overpass of the interstate.

"Frau, that was diabolical!" Gino said. "I didn't know you had it in you."

"Oh, that's just a start," she said. "I'm working my way up to baby seals!"

"What do you think he's going to tell the cops?" Viper looked around nervously.

"He's not going to tell them the truth, that's for sure. He will probably blame it on gang members or some issue with someone in the 'hood, but he is not going to admit that he got strung up over two kittens. How would that affect his macho quotient—to admit that he killed two helpless kittens? First of all, in Texas, cruelty to animals is a felony, and he can't risk going to jail, so he's going to clam up. Second, his buddies will never let him hear the end of it if he admits a one hundred pound woman tricked him. He's going to have to lie or say nothing."

She was right. The morning news was full of speculation about the man who was rescued hanging upside down from an overpass after numerous people passing underneath reported seeing him. His ordeal did not last long, but it was enough to make a believer of him.

All he would say is, "There are dark and deadly forces at work in this world, and I don't want to cross anymore of them."

When Frau returned the car to Danny the next day, he looked at the front end and said, "You didn't tell me there would be damage."

"I didn't tell you there wouldn't be, either." She laughed and handed him $500. "It was worth it. Let me know if it costs more." She walked away, humming "Dirty deeds, Done Dirt Cheap . . . "

4

After Frau dropped Gino off that night, he went straight to his room and locked the door, but he knew he wasn't going to get any sleep. The adrenaline rush was just too strong. Despite the nagging feeling that they had done something criminal, he felt exhilarated. He was ready to go out and conquer the world ! He felt invincible! Pacing back and forth in his small room, he felt caged and wanted to break out! He decided to go for a ride. His decision was based partly on his desire to make sure that Gigi was all right and partly to see the fruits of his labor. As he drove the few blocks from his house to the highway overpass, his mind was racing: The expression on Gigi's face right before they lowered him from the overpass was something he'd never forget. It was priceless. He'd never seen sheer terror in a person confronted with imminent demise. It was so pathetic, it was almost funny. But at the same time, Gino felt pity for the unsuspecting guy and hoped that he was okay.

As Gino approached the highway intersection, he saw the flashing lights of rescue vehicles and police cars. They had the whole north-bound side of the highway shut off. Gino decided to stay on the access road across the highway and drove slowly so that he could see whether it was a rescue or recovery scene. He could definitely see an ambulance, but was Gigi already in it or about to be loaded? He didn't want to seem suspicious, so he decided to pull into the Jack-in-the-Box twenty-four hour drive-thru and order something. At the moment, eating was out of the question, but purchasing something would afford him the opportunity to park in their lot and watch the events across the highway unfold.

Oh, yeah, he thought. *There's the gurney. Is Gigi on it?* He could see attendants on either side of the gurney rolling it toward the ambulance's open doors. *Yeah, there they go. Looks like they're loading him into the ambulance. I don't see a body bag; I guess he's alive. Yeah, there's the top of his head. I guess they'd have his head covered with a sheet or something if he was dead. Right?* Somewhat reassured, he started his car and pulled out of the lot slowly, still watching the surreal scene. *Boy, those people stuck on the highway must be really annoyed, especially the ones further back who can't see what's causing the back-up. I'm sure they are really pissed off!*

At that moment, it occurred to him that all of this confusion was partly his fault! The ambulance, police, fire trucks, the traffic jam, the flashing lights—he did this! Suddenly, he felt powerful. He was overwhelmed with confidence and machismo. Nothing could stop him! It was intoxicating. He wanted more. Then, just as suddenly, he felt tired—more exhausted than he had felt in his whole life.

He slowly headed for home, his mind still racing. He found himself hoping for another adventure—sooner rather than later. He still wasn't sure of Gigi's condition, but hoped he had survived, relatively unscathed, from his ordeal. True, he needed this lesson, and Gino hoped it would make a lasting impression. But Gino couldn't wait for the next "project." He pulled into the driveway at his dark house, put the car into park and slowly walked to the front door.

Man, am I tired. I'm going to sleep like a dead man. I'm definitely going to need to step up my game. Work out more. Build my endurance. Learn to swim. He hoped he wouldn't wake anyone in his house. He was in no mood to field questions. His thoughts were too chaotic to give satisfactory answers.

As he crawled into bed and closed his eyes, a thought occurred to him, and he reached into his nightstand and pulled out an object he hadn't touched in years—his rosary. "Father, forgive me, for I have sinned." His voice trailed away as he fell asleep.

The next morning, determined to fulfill his resolution of the night before, Gino left early for a workout at the karate school where he earned his black belt. He felt that he needed not only a strenuous workout but also the mental discipline that came with practicing karate. As he left home, he nonchalantly pitched something into the trash can. Walking purposefully to his truck, he started softly singing his favorite Foreigner song, "Feelin' down and dirty, feelin' kind of mean . . . I've been from one to the other extreme . . . "

Jackson, on the other hand, had a reaction to the Gigi incident that was not unexpected. The moment he got to his room, he "flopped" on his knees and began praying. "Father God, I come to you most humbly, seeking forgiveness for this and my many sins. I pray that you will ease my troubled mind and give me the strength to do your will and not to stray from the path of righteousness. I pray that you will surround Gigi with the angels of mercy, bless and protect him. Keep him safe. In Jesus' name I pray, Amen."

Surprised by his own lack of conviction, Jackson continued to pray off and on—sometimes for guidance, sometimes for Gigi's safety—until the early morning when he finally fell asleep and got some respite from his troubled thoughts. Yet, like Gino, he did feel empowered and reluctantly admitted to himself that he was looking forward to the next project. That there would be a next project, he was certain. Frau was just getting started.

Later that day, a trash collector noticed something shiny in a trash can on his route and leaned in to inspect it. Surprised to find a beautifully wrought religious object, he quickly grabbed it from the refuse, dropped the rosary into his pocket, and then looked around to see if anyone had seen him. He wondered who would throw away such a beautiful thing.

5

It was only a matter of days before Frau reconvened the Trifecta. Once they arrived at her house, she filled them in on what they already knew—what the world knew: A beloved rhino had been lured from a sanctuary and killed by a dimwitted American hunter named Jeff Atkins. And not just any rhino—a magnificent, black rhino that was part of a study. He was such a perfect specimen and had sired so many offspring at a crucial juncture for the rhino population that he was known as "The Unicorn." He was magical. And the rhino had suffered for hours after this so-called master hunter merely wounded him with a crossbow. The world was outraged, and Frau was itching to take immediate action.

"This guy has got to pay!" she fumed. "What an idiot! He lured the rhino, blinded it with a bright light, shot it with a crossbow at close range and still didn't kill it? This is a travesty—a crime against nature! Do you know that there are less than 5,000 black rhinos left in the world? And now all the pundits will argue over his right to hunt versus the sanctuary's right to protect, and he'll probably get off with a big fine which will mean nothing to him and maybe a suspension of his license. But his arrogance in the face of world-wide condemnation is egregious. He says it's the guide's fault. He claims he didn't know the rhino was part of a study. He didn't know he was in a protected area. Blah. Blah. Blah. He's an idiot, but his arrogance is what's gonna bring him down."

Gino and Jackson shot quizzical looks at each other. "How so, Frau?" Gino asked. They knew there would be no arguing with her.

"Because we're going to lure the Great Hunter in the same way that he lured the rhino. His arrogance is going to enable us to ensnare him. Did you hear what that talk show host said about the hunter? He's a fancy-ass corporate lawyer, you know." She was unaware that she was rambling. "Anyway, this guy was ranting about the rhino's death, and he said, 'If you have so much trouble getting an erection that you have to kill something, there's a pill for that,' and I just mentally applauded him, and I thought, 'He's right.' It's all about power and machismo and ego with this guy. And that's what we need to exploit. You know he's closed his legal practice in Colorado and gone into hiding. But there are ways to get to him, and that's what we're going to do."

"What do you mean 'we'?" Jackson asked. "What do you have in mind this time?"

"Did you ever read a short story called 'The Most Dangerous Game'?"

"Oh, yeah," Gino replied. "A hunter gets bored with killing animals; they're no longer a challenge, so he decides to find prey that is logical and can employ reason to prevail in the hunt. Uh Oh." He looked at Jackson. "You don't mean . . . ?"

"Oh, yes, but I do. We're going to find him, lure him and make him wish he'd never picked up a crossbow."

She looked at both young men. "Listen, Jackson. I know you're uncomfortable with this. And I respect that. You can bow out if you want to, but I need you to use your networking expertise to find this guy—to get the ball rolling. I told you a long time ago that you would be able to go with me only so far—that your moral, ethical being wouldn't let you go all the way. I get that. Your mission is to save people; mine is to save animals . If I need to put it in context for you, how about this: On the very first page of The Bible, the very first page in the book of Genesis, God gave man dominion over the fish of the sea, the fowl of the air, and the beasts of the field. That means we have to protect animals. It's a mandate from God. And since someone dropped that ball, I feel justified in going after this criminal. I don't want him to get off with a slap on the wrist for some technicality. Just find him for me. Please," she urged.

"All right, Frau. You know I wouldn't do this for anyone but you." He heaved a fretful sigh.

"And I appreciate that. Now, let's get busy. Dante's ninth circle is waiting."

On the drive back to Oak Cliff, Gino discussed the plan with Jackson, "Do you think Frau is unraveling? I mean, she really seems pissed—more so than usual."

"Unraveling?" Jackson scoffed. "I think she's looking at 'unraveling' in the rear view mirror. She might be certifiable. I still don't know what her plan is, but I don't think she'll go easy on this guy. I think she wants to do more than teach him a lesson. And I have to decide how far my ethics will let me go with this. I mean, I love Frau and all, but I'm too pretty for prison." He smiled his ridiculously toothy grin. "What do you think?"

Gino shrugged. "I'm all in. I know it will be a bumpy ride, but I agree with her: Jeff Atkins needs to pay for what he did to that rhino. And I'm willing to facilitate . . . "

Jackson started with hunting websites. Jeff Atkins was all over them. His Facebook page had been taken down, but hunting clubs still had pictures posted of him with his past kills. It was disgusting. This guy was a thrill-killer, and Jackson could already imagine other hunters taking up the mantle in his defense: *The herd needs to be culled. Old animals will starve to death. It's kinder to kill them, etc., etc., ad nauseum.*

After reading virtually everything there was to know about the rhino-killer, Jackson proceeded to blogs to see how hunters were responding to the outrage over the killing of The Unicorn. Surprisingly, many die-hard hunters were violently opposed to his "relied-on-the-guide" defense. They fumed that it was no excuse. That rhino was tagged, something that would have been immediately obvious. They berated him for making responsible hunters look bad. They derided his bungling of a clean kill. They disparaged his insistence on taking the rhino's head and skin, demanding that he return the felonious artifacts to the government of Namibia. They did not feel he had earned the right to display the items with his other big game trophies, which were now questionable as well.

Biologists were also weighing in, saying that the loss of the herd's patriarch would result in the deaths of his male offspring, at the mercy of other rhinos trying to move in and assume leadership of the herd. It was a disaster all the way around with biological repercussions for the balance of hierarchy.

And still the safari clubs were insisting that change is good, and that the rhino's death might actually have a positive effect in the long run. After all, they said, "The Unicorn was already ten years old. Maybe it was the right time for him to step aside and let a younger, more virile patriarch assume leadership and secure a new, stronger dynasty."

And the lawyer was still offering a lame apology that he didn't realize he "took" a rhino that was part of a study, to which the talk show host, overcome with emotion in his discourse, castigated him: "You 'take' an aspirin. You KILLED a rhino!"

Oh, yes, the "incident" spurred a national uproar—an international condemnation of the American who killed The Unicorn. There was no lack of information. Jackson just needed to zero in on the trace information that would lead him to the lawyer's hideout. Jackson found one comment suggesting that the lawyer owned property further north— up in "real hunting country." He posited that, since the guy had $40,000 to throw away on a hunting expedition, he probably owned a big, sprawling weekend home on one of the lakes in the north of the state. All he had to do was search county records; nothing was confidential anymore. So he acquainted himself with hunting lodges privately owned in areas highly coveted by inveterate hunters, until he ran across one in an upscale resort named "Quail Run." It boasted of master suites, marble countertops, Mexican tile floors, spas and three car underground garages for the family cars and all-terrain vehicles cherished by backwoods enthusiasts. Jackson thought the underground garage would be a good place to hide out.

After delving into the resort's public records, Jackson discovered a listing for "J. Atkins." Even better, it listed the name and number of the property's caretaker: Samuel Stevens. Jackson called Frau with the info. She sounded pleased.

"But, Frau, what's the next step? Do you want me to go to Colorado and bring him back? You know, I can't kidnap someone and take them across state lines. That would be some serious jail time."

"Don't I know it! No, we're going to take another approach—one that will bring him to us. Here's what I want you to do: Get in touch with the caretaker. Tell him you're interested in buying property there. Ask him about other property owners in the guise of knowing who your future neighbors might be. If you can gain his confidence, he might give up some information that will help us."

"Will do," Jackson said. "Anything else?"

"No," she replied. "If I can confirm where he is, especially if we can get an email address or something that he's still discreetly using on social media, we can start setting him up."

"Frau, I'm willing to get the info you need, but I'm really reluctant to be a part of any vigilante group."

"You know, 'vigilante' is such an ugly term," she mused. "I think 'crusader' better captures the spirit of my endeavor. However, I know your ethical quandary. I'm not insensitive to your situation. Still . . . " she paused. "Back to The Bible. You know the Ten Commandments, I am sure."

"Of course."

"Well, one of the Commandments is 'Thou shalt not kill.' Am I right?"

"Yes," he replied warily.

"It doesn't say, 'Thou shalt not kill man,' does it? I mean, it's just 'Thou shalt not kill.' Period. Right? So, to me, that's a mandate not to kill anything. Literally. That's why I don't kill spiders and wasps or whatever. I re-locate them. You know that. You've seen me do it."

"Many times." He chuckled, recalling Frau gingerly trying to trap spiders on windowsills.

"Well, to me, it was a sin for Jeff Atkins to kill The Unicorn. First, he violated a covenant we have with God to care for his animal kingdom, and second, he violated a commandment. He's a sinner, pure and simple – an evil man who deserves punishment."

"But The Bible also says, 'Vengeance is mine, saith the Lord'." Jackson sounded as if he were on the verge of delivering a sermon.

"Okay, and 'an eye for an eye'. You see, we can go back and forth all day about this. No one's going to win this debate. I'm counting on God to exact the ultimate punishment. I just want to do my part to make Atkins' life on earth a living hell."

"Frau, when you're right, you're right. There's no arguing with you. I will contact the gentleman at Quail Run and sound him out. You can focus on the rest of the plan."

"Thank you, Jackson. That's why I call you the 'voice of reason'."

For her part, Frau put in a call to an old friend:

"Hey, Miss Pam. What's up?"

"Ain't nothing, Baby Girl. What's up with you? Your pussy need to be shaved again?"

Frau laughed. "No, not yet, thanks." Frau Geiger was no prude. She frequently dropped the "f-bomb" and occasionally labeled someone an "m-f-er," but the "P" word was normally like fingernails on the chalkboard to her. With Pam, though, it had become a long-running joke. A typical conversation would be . . .

"Is this Pam, the purveyor of the pussy parlor?"

"Yes, ma'am, we will shave your pussy in no time, satisfaction guaranteed."

"Okay, that's good, because my pussy is looking really ragged."

"I bet it does; it's been a while since I got after it with a trimmer! Ha-Ha!"

Pam, a former vet tech and now the receptionist for a prominent veterinarian, was the only person Frau trusted to shave her two Maine Coon cats when they got matted.

At least once a year, she would prevail upon Pam to shave them. The only problem was the scheduling because Pam was hard to pin down. Sometimes Trixie and Heidi had to wait weeks before Pam could work them in. She only shaved them on Thursdays, because she got off at noon. Her standard operating procedure was to shave the cats, which often included her Persian, Vinnie, then race home to take a shower. Shaving cats is a really hairy job.

"Well," Pam said, "If it's not the cats, do you need some orange-cranberry scones from Trader Joe's?"

"No, well, yes, that would be great, but it's not the reason I called. I need a favor."

"For you, anything, Chica. Name it."

"There's this guy . . . " Frau began.

"Say no more. I'll do it!"

"Hey, you don't even know what it is! It's kind of evil," Frau said in a tone that was vaguely sinister.

"Even better. I want to help."

"Okay, but I'm telling you, it's questionable."

"When have you ever known me to back away from a challenge? You know what a bitch I can be."

"Exactly," Frau laughed. "That's why you're the first person—the only person really—that I thought of."

"Well, what's the deal and, more to the point, why me?"

"Pam, I have seen you in action—in the vet's office—in the vet's office, for Christ's sake! You wrap men around your little finger so fast and so smooth, they don't even know what hit them. I mean, ornery old men, who probably can't even get an erection, come to life when they're around you. They're like little boys with a schoolyard crush. You are mesmerizing. You look at them like they're the only man on the planet, and all of their barriers melt away! They are, literally, putty in your devious hands."

"Ha, ha, no kidding. Some of those guys look like they're having a heart attack. They just love the attention." Pam was well aware of the power she had over men.

"Oh, it's more than that. You are seducing them with your eyes, your voice. It's perfect for my plan."

"How so?"

"I want you to call Jeff Atkins and use your wiles on him to lure him to Texas."

"Jeff Atkins? The rhino-killer?" Pam sounded incredulous.

"The same."

"Holy crap! This is big!"

"Yes, it's major. I warned you." Frau chuckled as she imagined the expression on Pam's face.

"All right. So exactly what is my role in this?"

"Well, you're going to tell him you're with a canned hunt outfit and get him to come out of hiding to participate in a canned hunt for a mountain lion down in the Hill Country."

"Via Skype?"

"How else? That should be more reassuring to him, seeing who he's dealing with. And at the same time, you'll be able to work your magic, using your visually seductive charms – those eyes, that sultry voice . . . "

"Oh, darling, you are giving me the big head."

"No, that's what I want you to give him. Just get him to agree to come to Texas."

"I'll get him to come in Texas."

"Don't go that far."

"No, I wouldn't let that weasel touch me. You know I talk a good game, but I have standards. But I'll do my part to get him here."

"When I grow up, I want to be just like you, Miss Pam." Frau laughed as she hung up.

7

After a lengthy phone conversation with Samuel Stevens, the caretaker at Quail Run, Jackson reported to Frau: "I got some interesting information from Mr. Stevens. He was beyond forthcoming. He confirmed that Jeff Atkins has a big cabin at the lake, but he is universally despised."

"Oh, really? Did he say why?"

"Pretty much. He's an arrogant guy with a lot of money and a questionable reputation for ethics in the hunting community. You know the area's gun and hunting enthusiasts feel like, if they play by the rules, everyone should. And Mr. Atkins doesn't. He bends and breaks rules, then brags about how he got away with it. He thinks he's untouchable because he's a fancy-ass lawyer."

"Yeah, I figured he was the kind who would get off on getting around the rules; he has a narcissistic quality about him, like rules don't apply to him, just to the 'common' folks."

"Oh, but Mr. Stevens was quick to give me Atkins' contact info. It's as if he wants the guy to get into trouble. The amazing thing is, he said that I'm the first person to contact him. It seems that everyone else is focused on Atkins' vacation home in Florida, but he's actually hiding out at his in-law's home. They have a cottage on their property where a groundskeeper normally lives, but he's on vacation so Atkins and his family are there. He said Atkins is really scared, and his wife is giving him hell for putting them in this position."

"Oh, that's excellent. I was hoping the little woman would be giving him the blues. I hope the guy is miserable."

"Well, what's the next step?"

"You got his contact information, so we need to create a bogus website promoting canned hunts in the Hill Country that will entice him out of hiding."

"You mean, I need to create a website," Jackson joked.

"Of course, you. You know I'm old-school. I don't have the know-how for technology like you young guys do. That website you set up for our educational foundation was beautiful. It was professional, detailed, informative . . . you thought of things that never would have occurred to me but just seemed so obviously integral to the product."

"Yes, that West Coast education has really paid off, but I am going to have to do a little research into—what did you call it—canned hunts?"

"Yes, it's a heinous business. I first became aware of it when Ann Richards was governor. I saw a video that infuriated and sickened me. A truck loaded with a big crate pulled up in an open field. A bunch of guys with rifles were standing around while two men unloaded the cage. Almost immediately, someone opened the door to the cage, a magnificent black panther ran out and was instantly shot by one of the so-called hunters! Where's the sport in that? Some asshole took home a trophy that never had a chance. It literally was just a matter of minutes. There's no telling how much that guy paid for that travesty. He probably went home and bragged to his buddies about what a great hunter he is! What a joke!"

"When I saw that, I immediately wrote to Ann Richards, urging her to put an end to it. I thought real hunters and anyone with a heart or sense of sportsmanship would be outraged. I basically got a form letter from her, saying she appreciated my concern and they were doing everything they could in Austin to put an end to such unjust acts. It was all bullshit. She was in the pocket of the good old boys' network. They control everything in Austin, and most of them are gun advocates and hunters themselves. And by the way, I think Richards was a hunting enthusiast as well, so it was all talk to shut me up. But I haven't forgotten, and I'm determined to shine a light on this crime."

"Wow, Frau. I never even heard of anything like that before."

"Yeah, they're great at sweeping things under the rug, especially when it's a big bucks operation like these canned hunts are. It seems like a lot of people profit from it. And remember, Jeff Atkins paid forty thousand to kill The Unicorn, so these people have deep pockets in addition to a complete lack of conscience. All of this macho stuff just feeds their egos."

"All right. I know what to do. I'll get the website set up, then contact Atkins with an offer he won't be likely to refuse."

"Right. Then, I'll set him up with my friend Pam for the sales pitch. If she can't get him to come to Texas for a sure-thing hunt, no one can."

8

While Jackson worked on the canned hunt website and Pam awaited further instructions, Frau made a few phone calls to friends in the Austin area. After having a couple of pleasant if unproductive conversations, she finally decided to call her old friend Morris Birnbaum.

"Hey, MoMo." His childhood name was known only to his inner circle. "Long time, no see. What's going on in your part of the world?"

"Baby Girl, where have you been? I've been thinking about calling you. Are you staying out of trouble?"

"Nah. But they haven't caught up with me yet," she laughed.

"So what's going on?" he asked directly. "Because I know you didn't call to talk politics."

"No, you're right about that. I need a favor."

"Of course, you do. What is it this time? You want to bring some of your students to the ranch?"

"No, not this time. It's more complicated than that. I want to prank a guy."

"Wow. I'd hate to be on your shit list. What did he do? Stand you up at the altar?"

"Oh, if only it were that simple. Have you heard of Jeff Atkins?"

"Who hasn't? He's all over the news. I'm not sure if I want to hear this."

"Well, you know he needs to have a good old-fashioned Texas ass-kickin'. I want to put him in the wilderness and see just how big and brave he isn't."

"Interesting. And?"

"Your ranch is big and wild, right in the middle of canned hunt central. The perfect spot for a spanking, if you ask me."

"Hold on now. You know I'm all for him getting his come-uppance, but I'm fixin' to make another run at the governor's office. I don't want to shoot myself in the foot by doing something illegal. " Momo was quiet as he thought the idea through. "How about this: The land adjacent to my property is federally protected. If we fly under the radar, you can use my property to stage your hunt over there and, hopefully, the federales won't swing through for a few days."

"Okay, that sounds perfect," she said. "I don't want you to get in any trouble. You know I'm your biggest supporter."

"Yeah, I'm going to need your help with my campaign, if you can tear yourself away from school long enough."

"Don't worry," she assured him. "I retired. I've got all kind of time for a good cause."

Frau especially liked MoMo because, unlike the good old boys, he was genuine and was an avid teacher- and animal-advocate. He actually ran an animal rescue organization out of his ranch. An author himself, he promoted literacy and was also a talented musician—a regular Renaissance man, Texas-style.

"Just keep me out of it or I won't have a chance in hell of getting into the governor's office. You know most of these boys around here are trigger-happy, dues-paying members of the NRA. They prize their deer leases and hunt anything that moves. Right now, we've got a problem with wild pigs. Those feral swine are breeding at record rates, and they're tearing up the environment. It's a real politically-charged issue. They want to fly over my ranch in helicopters, shooting the pigs. I said, 'No fuckin' way!' but it's all I can do to keep them at bay. They are relentless, but I don't want that on my conscience."

"I know what you mean. It's a tricky road to navigate. I know they're invasive and out-of-control, but shooting them from helicopters is really nasty business."

"It is, but the hogs are mean and big. I'm telling you, it's bad for people who plant crops and bad for the ecosystem, but they're just doing what pigs do."

That's why Frau liked MoMo. He didn't espouse the party line or try to be politically correct; he was a free thinker who did what he believed was right. He actually had a conscience and wasn't driven by the bottom line like so many politicians. He was as worried about the feral pigs' welfare as he was about their environmental impact. That's why his political campaigns were neither Democrat nor Republican; he always ran as an independent. He wasn't in anyone's pocket, but that also made him a long shot. She certainly didn't want to compromise his campaign.

"Okay, then," she said. "Once everything is confirmed, I'll be back in touch. Can you scout the area and see the best place for our little game? I mean, I want it to be really wild and really rugged, so Mr. Rhino-Killer gets a dose of his own medicine. We want scorpions, tarantulas and big ol' rattlers. The more, the better."

"Oh," he laughed. "Don't worry. We've got those in spades."

9

In the meantime, Gino was getting restless. Although he knew that it would take some extensive preliminary work to set up the Jeff Atkins project, he was eager to get busy. Waiting around for responses to his job applications was frustrating as well, so he decided to do a little investigating of his own.

After Googleing "animal cruelty cases" and "animal cruelty websites," he was staggered and sickened by what he encountered. Videos in which animals are crushed to death for people's online amusement was something he wanted to address, but he had to put that on the back burner; the logistics of sabotaging websites was monumental and the people who ran them were all over the globe. But it was definitely going on his 'to-do" list. Animal fetishists? He didn't need that in his head. *God, what could that entail?* He was sure he didn't want to know.

What caught his attention was a major university up north that was being targeted by an animal ethics group for its continuing program of animal experimentation, which amounted to torture. Funded by a national health agency, this university had apparently been under scrutiny for years for its heinous cruelty to its experimental subjects but persisted in using animals in questionable and largely useless studies. The website featured clandestine photos taken in one of the labs, showing cats with electrodes permanently attached to their skulls with screws. The cats' discomfort and distress was so blatant, it was sickening. The ethics group had obtained copies of lab reports as well in which the cats' pain was noted in a very clinical, indifferent manner. The note documented the cats' depression, weight loss, level of pain, and the fact that they were later euthanized and beheaded. It was horrific that researchers could ignore such obvious signs of distress.

Anyone who knew Frau was bound to be exposed to a certain amount of information about animal cruelty. Still, Gino could see now that she had not given them the real dirt, and there was plenty of that to go around. Something needed to be done—and fast.

He started doing some calculations. The round trip from Dallas to the university was a little over 1,000 miles. His truck averaged 756 miles per tank. He would need to stop once each way to refuel. He'd need cash—no credit card trails. He figured the trip each way would be 16 hours. That was nothing. His trips to Mexico were usually 18-24 hours. Traveling non-stop was a way of life for him. He'd stock up on Red Bull and caffeine and just go for it. The tricky part was isolating the offices of these animal torturers from the lab area. He didn't want to cause further harm to animals already under siege. He just wanted to send a message to these cold-hearted individuals who could so callously mistreat animals—all in the name of dubious scientific research.

Reaching for the calendar, he selected early Saturday morning for his departure with the intent of being back by Sunday afternoon. He might have to stop to rest for a couple of hours at one of those roadside parks or maybe a

24-hour Wal-Mart—no, they probably had surveillance cameras. That meant when he stopped for gas, he'd better find one of those out-of-the-way, low-tech gas stations with no security cameras.

He started making a list of things he needed: extra gasoline cans, water, an alarm clock, black clothes, gloves, a ball cap, Red Bull, cokes, energy bars, map—normally, he would rely on his cell phone's navigational system, but he had decided to leave the cell phone behind—a risky decision, but he didn't want anyone tracking him—rope, duct tape, some homemade incendiary devices—he knew that materials class would come in handy some day—cable, wire, check the spare in the truck. He knew he was leaving something out, but he hadn't determined the exact method. This was so fresh to him; it challenged him and piqued his intellectual capabilities.

He wasn't sure what Frau would think of his plan, especially with the Jeff Atkins thing looming, so he decided not to tell her. She was busy anyway trying to lay the groundwork for The Unicorn's killer to get his "reprimand." *Yeah*, he thought. *This is best kept to myself. What's that old saying? 'Two can keep a secret if one is dead'? That's my new philosophy. I hope I don't forget to take that Longhorn trailer hitch off my truck. I want to be as inconspicuous as possible.*

10

A few days later, Frau called Jackson. "Viper, how's everything coming with the website? Have you got it up and running?"

"Of course, Frau. I was just going to call you. Do you want me to come show you what I've got?" Jackson sounded unusually proud of himself.

"Yeah," she replied. "I can't wait to see it. Do you think you can swing by Gino's and bring him, too?"

"I don't know where he is. I've been trying to get in touch with him all weekend. He's not responding."

"Hmmm. I had the same problem. I texted him yesterday, but got no answer. It's not like him." Frau ignored the beeping of an incoming call after checking to be sure it wasn't Gino.

"I know. But I'll run by his house. It's not out of the way. Maybe his sister will tell me where he is.

"Okay, but I won't hold my breath. Just bring your laptop. I want to get going with this canned hunt thing."

"Will do." He signed off.

When Jackson arrived at Frau's house, she was surprised to see that he had Gino in tow.

"Hey, where'd you find him?" she jokingly asked.

"I thought he'd left the country. Man, you look like hell," she said, directing her comment to Gino.

"Oh, yeah, I just got back from visiting my cousin at Texas Tech. His girlfriend dumped him on Facebook. He was having a rough time, so I went out to distract him."

"I thought he graduated from Tech last May." She looked at Gino quizzically.

"Oh, no, actually, he's graduating in December. Anyway, I just barely got back when Jackson pulled up. I was getting stuff out of my truck."

"Well, you must have driven straight through. You look like you need a nap."

"Yeah," he agreed. He shook his head in an effort to wake up.

"Did Jackson tell you we've been trying to get in touch with you?"

"Yeah, I've been having trouble with my phone—dropping calls and stuff. I think it was too many dead zones—something. I need to take it in to see what's wrong."

"You mean that new phone you just got this summer? What was it? A Nexus 6 or something? It's been giving you problems?" She sounded skeptical.

"Uh, yeah, off and on. I just think it got bad this past week. I'm going to take it in." Gino tapped his finger nervously on the table.

"Oh, well, I hope you get it straightened out soon. You're going to need a dependable phone for this next project."

Jackson interrupted. "Oh, oh, Frau. Did you hear about that explosion at that university up north where they do all those animal experiments?"

"Yeah, that's what I was trying to text Gino about yesterday. I heard it on the evening news. It reminded me of that young couple they arrested in Utah during the summer. Apparently, they had been going across country to these facilities where they do horrible experiments on animals of all kinds. They were breaking into the labs, freeing the animals and taking them to rescue groups. But they were arrested, so this couldn't have been them."

"Evidently not. No one is claiming responsibility for it," he said.

"Well, it's not like ISIS or someone is going to take credit. It's clearly a strike for justice for the animals, and that particular facility is notorious for its long-term experimental program. A major animal rights group has been trying to shut them down for a long time, but I guess it's harder when they're funded by the health institute." She looked at Gino. "Did you hear about it?"

"Uh, no, no, uh . . . I've kind of been out of touch—you know, the phone issue." He avoided her gaze.

Frau looked sharply at him. He was being uncharacteristically quiet, not his usual convivial self at all.

"Uh huh. Well, it's a victory for the animals. The good thing is, whoever did this was careful to only blow up the annex where records and supplies are stored. Of course, they can just go to any computer and download recent records, but a lot of stuff that was in that building was some surreptitious, off-the-record stuff and documents that had never been archived. It's a big set-back for them and their program. A lot of that data is what they base their grant applications on, so it's back to square one for them and, hopefully, they won't want to start all over again. Animal rights groups are delighted."

She looked directly at Gino. "I can't believe you didn't hear about this. Tech can't be that far off the grid. They do have radio and television, right?

"Of course. It's just that I was focused on Jorge, trying to cheer him up."

"Okay. Jackson, let's see what you've got." Frau glanced at her cellphone and said, "Wait. I need to take this call."

"Geiger speaking. No, I can't talk right now. I'll call you later. Ok, no problem." She looked at Gino and Jackson.

"Who was that? Your boyfriend?" Jackson chuckled.

"One of them," she said, smirking. "All right. Let's do this."

Jackson produced his laptop, and they gathered around to see the fruits of his labor.

Entitled "Lone Star Guided Hunts," the website gave an overview of the facility and featured pictures from past hunts—with weekend hunters and their so-called "trophies." It showed smiling people in ATVs loaded with equipment and supplies—destined for two and three-day expeditions into the rugged Hill Country outside Austin. Included was a laundry list of prices for services provided—the more rugged experience involved camp-outs in tents while the upscale hunts involved staying in plush cabins with all the amenities, but it was just window dressing. The hunters could cook-out and drink fine wine with their steaks and sleep in big, comfy beds, but the actual "hunt" would take place in a short span—morning or afternoon, your choice. The prey's normal feeding, hunting, sleeping schedules would not enter into their pursuit at all. Because there was no pursuit. Just a terrified animal unloaded from a truck and shot as it exited a cage.

"Wow, this is impressive," Frau remarked. "Where did you get all these photos?"

"Well, there are several websites where you can download images like these and, if Jeff Atkins is smart and does his research, he might recognize some of them, but I'm betting he's not that smart. I'm counting on his gullibility and his unabated desire to add to his collection of trophies to lure him in. The fact that I sent this online brochure to his personal email should lend to its authenticity, don't you think?"

"Where'd you get his personal email address?" Gino asked.

"From the caretaker at his weekend retreat."

"Why would he give the guy's email to you? He doesn't even know you."

"I think he wants this guy to get in trouble. Didn't you hear? Namibia is not going to extradite Atkins. All charges against him have been dropped."

"Damn," Gino said. "There's just no justice."

"Yes, that's why what we're going to do is all the more important. This guy needs to know that actions have consequences. If the court doesn't want to go after him, it's up to us. All we have to do now is to wait for him to respond. I don't think it will be long." Frau looked at her cellphone and hit the "reject" button.

"No, especially now that he thinks he's off the hook. He'll be eager to get back to killing magnificent animals. Let me know as soon as you hear from him."

"Will do, Frau. In the meantime, I think I'd better get Cobra home so he can get some sleep. He looks beat."

"I am. That drive was long, and I haven't had any sleep. I feel like I could sleep for a week," Gino said.

Although his body was exhausted, his mind was racing from thoughts that he had yet to process. He wanted to just get away from everyone and debrief. Then it would be on to the next phase.

As Gino and Jackson waved good-bye to Frau, she could not help but think, *I wonder if my little buddy Gino has gone rogue on me?* She smiled at the thought.

11

On the drive home from Frau's house, Gino thought Jackson would never stop talking. His head was pounding from lack of sleep and food. Normally, he found Jackson quite entertaining, but this time, he was just relieved when Jackson finally dropped him off in the late afternoon.

As he passed his truck, he thought, *I really need to unload everything*, but fatigue was telling him a different story. He went in and headed straight for bed—no shower, no change of clothes; he just flopped on the bed and sank into a deep sleep. It wasn't until almost noon the next day that he finally woke up. He felt horrible. He knew he needed to eat something, but the thought of food repulsed him. Maybe some Gatorade would help. He went to the refrigerator, got a bottle of G2 and drank greedily. *No doubt I'm dehydrated. Why do I feel so tired? Oh yeah*, he thought groggily. *The trip.* Suddenly, he brightened a little. *Yeah, the trip. Man, that was great!*

He started thinking back to Friday night and how apprehensive he had been about going. *What's the worst thing that can happen? The cops stop me for some reason and then what? There won't be anything incriminating. They can't search the truck without due cause and even if they do, what will they find? Work-related supplies and materials. Mostly. At that point, I can just turn around and go home. Mission not accomplished, but no harm done.* Resolved, he went to bed, determined to carry out his plan.

He left at 4:00 AM and headed north. When he walked out of his house, there was a chill in the air, the promise of fall and colder weather. With a twinge of regret, he recalled passing the vacant lot where Lyn's SnoCones always stands in the summer and how Frau says her closing up is the harbinger of winter. It was true. He zipped up his jacket and put on his ball cap, then started the truck and backed out. *Well*, he thought. *This is it. I hope I've covered all my bases and anticipated every possible problem I might encounter.*

By that time, he had memorized his entire route, right down to the towns on the highway that were regarded by frequent travelers as speed traps. There was no way to avoid them; he would just have to be super-cautious. No driving with a lead foot on the open road. Sixteen hours would put him at his destination around 10:00 PM, which was perfect. He already knew the general area where he would stop to refuel; it was just a matter of finding an old-school service station with no security cameras.

As the sun rose, Gino began to settle into the comfort of the drive. The scenery was nothing to get excited about, but this was the first time he had ever headed north instead of south on I-35, so he looked forward to the challenges ahead.

Gino quickly fell into the routine and cadence of highway travel; I-35 was usually heavily populated by eighteen-wheelers, but it was lighter on the weekend, so his trip proved uneventful for the first eight hours. When his fuel gauge was down to an eighth of a tank, he started paying attention to the roadside gas stations. No Exxon or

FasGas; too risky. He wanted a little mom-and-pop stop in the middle of nowhere – in between big city gas stations.

Finally, just at dusk, he spotted one that looked promising. It was a small town with a few buildings clustered around the highway exit, including a small gas station with two pumps, a restroom and a little convenience store. Pulling in, he noticed one other car in the small parking lot. After he filled his tank, he made a quick stop in the restroom before heading to the clerk to pay. When he pushed the door open, he had to look around to find the attendant, a tired-looking, middle-aged man with a lumberjack shirt, wire-rimmed glasses and a bald spot. *Kinda looks like Ben Franklin*, he thought, smiling. Approaching the guy with a "Hey, what's going on?" Gino suddenly felt a chill. But this time, the weather had nothing to do with it. His natural instinct told him something wasn't right. Instantly, he was on high alert. Walking closer to the clerk, he said, "I put forty bucks in. Can you change a fifty?"

The clerk didn't look at him but just nodded. Gino tapped his finger on the glass countertop to get the guy's attention. When he looked up, Gino raised his eyebrows as if to ask, "Is everything okay?" The man quickly looked away and started to open the cash register.

It was then that Gino caught a glimpse of something in a mirrored display case. Behind him, to the right, he could see a man, his back flattened against an end cap, trying to avoid being seen. Almost without thinking, Gino grabbed a Swiss army knife from the display case and flung it quickly over his right shoulder. It struck the glass dairy case near the hidden figure, making such a clatter that he was momentarily startled and distracted from watching Gino who, taking advantage of the opportunity, rushed the guy with his full body force, tackling him and sending him sprawling. A hand gun came out of his pocket in the melee and slid across the floor. The clerk ran over as Gino was struggling to restrain the man and asked, "What do you want me to do? Call the police?"

"No," Gino yelled. "Just get me something I can restrain him with—rope, zip ties, duct tape—anything. And hurry!"

The clerk ran behind the counter and returned with some rope, but Gino said, "That's not enough! Get more or get something else. I don't care. Just hurry!" The guy was bigger than Gino and was fighting to extricate himself from Gino's hold, but Gino was determined that the creep wasn't going to get away. He wasn't even sure what the guy's intention was, but the gun indicated it wasn't good. The guy was sprawled face down on the floor with Gino on top of him for what seemed an endless time before the clerk finally showed up with more rope.

"Okay, while I have my knee in his back, see if you can tie his hands behind him and triple or quadruple tie it. Then get his feet." As the would –be robber continued to fight and curse at Gino, threatening to track him down "wherever he came from and blow him up," Gino was getting more and more agitated. "You're kind of pissing me off now. I'm not your bitch, so if you don't shut up, I'm going to get a hot poker and shove it up your dumb ass!"

"I wasn't doin' nothin'," the guy protested. "What'd you jump me for?"

"I don't know. Maybe it's the fact that you were hiding, which is a little suspicious—and then there's the gun."

"Oh, well, if you're going to jump everyone with a gun, you're going to stay real busy! This is hunting country." The guy sneered at Gino.

"You hunt with a handgun?" Gino snorted.

"Just let me go, man. I haven't done nothin'!"

After securing the guy's hands and feet, Gino turned to the clerk, "You can do what you want. Call the cops. Let him go. I don't care. I'm outta here," and he turned to go.

Over his shoulder, he said, "I still think his intentions were bad, but it's your call. Do me a favor, though, and leave me out of any statements you make. I'm just passing through. I don't have time for a lot of questions and explanations. I'm just trying to help."

"Okay, dude, whatever you say," the clerk responded. "You were right about him, though. He was planning to rob me. He'd already pointed his gun at me when you drove up. You saved my ass."

Gino laughed and said, "Compliments of Cobra, man!" Gino recalled the Lynyrd Skynyrd song lyrics, "Guns ain't good for nothin'. Why don't we take 'em all and throw 'em to the bottom of the sea . . . "

Cranking up the truck, he thought. *That was surreal. Who would have thought that I would have the bad luck to choose the one place that had a hold-up in progress and no security?* He laughed at the irony. *It's probably the same reason the robber picked it; it looked like an easy target.*

By 10:00 PM, Gino was exiting the highway and heading for Bruce Hall on McConnell Street. Luckily, the university was just off the highway—less chance of getting lost in a maze of suburbia. He had committed the layout of the campus to memory so he wouldn't waste time looking for his target. *All right, this should be it. Right turn on McConnell; second building on the right.* He recognized Bruce Hall immediately from the breezeway connecting it to the science lab where the animals were housed. All he had to do was find an inconspicuous place to park, get his materials out of the truck and put them into action. He found a good place close to Bruce, partly shielded by a big dumpster, and started getting everything ready. He had made some simple incendiary devices at home; all he needed to do was add some gasoline, mount them on his drones and deploy them to the building. Gino had scrutinized the university's official website and calendar to insure that no one would be in the building on Saturday.

He hated to lose the drones that he and his roommates had made to compete in drone races in Austin. They were special, like children, but he felt he had to sacrifice them in the interest of expediency. He simply didn't have time to build more before he left. *It's for a good cause*, he kept telling himself; still, he was filled with regret. *They're sweet little UAVs*, he thought, as he prepared them for their mission. His navigational goggles would be useless in the dark; he would have to rely on the drones' lights to guide them. Before he launched them, he gave them a little kiss for good luck and sent them, laden with flammable goods, to Bruce Hall. His objective was to incinerate Bruce Hall and all of its horrific experimental records. *There they go*, he lamented and then turned his attention to the task at hand, getting them to their terminal destination.

He intended to send one high; the building was only three stories; and the other, low on the back side of the hall. Now, he was fully focused on insuring the success of his mission. *One chance*, he kept telling himself. *No do-overs*. His drones were performing like storm troopers, the way they had when they won the regional competition in Austin. They were responsive, quick, and accurate. He was pleased with their performance.

The first one reached its target on the corner of the roof. The second took longer to reach the back of the building. Both were on course. As soon as they were in position, Gino hit the "deploy" button, and the sparks began to fly.

At that point, Gino raced back to his truck, threw the remaining materials in the back and took off. He knew he didn't have time to waste. Even though it was a Saturday and few people were around, it wouldn't take long for the fire to attract attention. He planned to be back on the highway headed south when that happened. *Don't look back. Just keep going.* In his rearview mirror, however, he saw the sky light up as the combustibles he concocted began to ricochet around the building, creating a domino effect. One flare-up followed another; it looked like Fourth of July fireworks pinwheeling. *That is just spectacular! Maybe I should go into pyrotechnics! I do enjoy an explosive light display!*

His light show took the whole town by surprise. They were so preoccupied assembling the volunteer fire department to battle the blaze, no one noticed the black truck speeding south on I-35.

12

Two days later, Jackson called Frau from his cell phone and said, "Good news. I got an email from Atkins. He's interested, but cautious. So far, he's just asking questions, wants clarification. He wants to be sure we're discreet."

"I don't blame him. He's been the subject of international scorn for three months now. I'd want to stay under the radar for a while, but his trigger finger must be itchy. He's an inveterate hunter, and he wants to get back in the game, the arrogant bastard. Oh, sorry, Jackson. I've got to watch my mouth."

"Don't worry, Frau. You know I've heard worse. So what's next?"

"Just keep reassuring him until he makes up his mind. Remind him of the advantages: It's in the U.S. – a big plus for him since Namibia has gone on record that he will no longer be given a license to hunt anything there. It's a sure thing with minimal effort on his part. And, most of all, it will provide him with the big rhino trophy he didn't get because the government refused to release The Unicorn's head and carcass for transport to the U.S. I am sure he wants some consolation."

"Right, Frau. So when do you want me to schedule the Skype meeting?"

"Don't be pushy. Act coy. Let him think he's calling all the shots 'cause that's how his big ego works. He likes to be in charge. You can suggest it for clarification purposes but let him request the time, then I'll call my little friend Pam, and she will lure him in."

"Do you think she can do that?" he asked.

"There's not a doubt in my mind. I've not met the man who is immune to her charm."

"Sounds interesting, Frau. Ok. I'll keep shoveling the bovine excrement at Atkins."

"You have such a refined way with words, Viper. You make me proud."

He laughed as he hung up.

Later that evening, he called Frau while she was feeding her menagerie and said, "Hey, Frau, you won't believe it, but Atkins is ready to set a date."

"Really?" she said, surprised. "I thought he'd wait a few days, maybe do a little research on the company or look for some reviews, but I guess I was second-guessing my own hypothesis about the size of his ego."

"Yeah, he's ready to go. Maybe he's smarting a little about being denied the rhino's head and carcass and wants to pre-empt his hunting buddies' taunts by getting his trophy head another way."

"Yeah, I'll have to put in calls to Momo and Pam to see how fast they can be ready. I'll get back to you."

"Okay," Jackson said. "The sooner, the better. He seems eager to go now."

Immediately, Frau called Pam and asked, "Hey, girl. Jackson just called and said Jeff Atkins is ready to negotiate the deal. Are you ready to deal with him?"

"Oh, yeah," Pam responded. "I've got my part down. I know exactly what to say to this guy. In fact, I can't wait."

"Excellent—because he wants to move up the timeline and I want to accommodate him. I just need to be sure you're on board and then get Jackson to set up the Skype meeting."

"Don't worry, Baby-Cakes. I've got this."

"I'll be in touch, like, real soon."

Next, she called Momo and said, "When can you be ready for us, because my guy is ready to go."

"No problem. I'll talk to the locals and make sure they steer clear of the staging area for a while. Just tell me when, and I'll take care of it."

"You're the best. I really owe you large."

"And don't forget it."

Two hours later, the Trifecta met at her house to finalize the plan. Sitting around the kitchen table, they relished the bean-and-cheese tamales that Frau's neighbor Rosie had brought to her.

"These are delicious," Gino wiped his mouth with the back of his hand.

"Rosie never disappoints," Frau agreed, biting into a juicy tidbit.

"What did you find out from Mo?" Jackson asked, helping himself to more salsa.

"He can be ready at a moment's notice, apparently. It seems he has some kind of unholy alliance with the people overseeing that protected area, and he's going to call them off whenever we set a date."

"That works in our favor, because I've been wondering how we were going to elude the authorities while we play." Jackson pushed his chair away from the table to avoid further temptation.

"Definitely. And Pam is good to go, too. But here's the problem: We need to really make this look good. When we pick him up at the airport, we have to sell the deal with a limo and driver and the whole show. But where are we going to get one? We can't bring anyone else in; it has to be one of you that picks him up."

"Oh, Frau, I meant to tell you, that's a problem," Jackson said. "He wants to drive in rather than fly. He's afraid people at the airport will recognize him."

"Look, Jackson, you're going to have to convince him that, in the interest of expediency, we need to get him here faster than he can drive. I don't want his abandoned car sitting around attracting attention."

"Excellent point. I will stress that in my next email—the expediency, I mean."

"As far as transportation from the airport goes, I got this," Gino said.

"How so?"

"Do you remember my cousin Juan, the one who roomed with me for a while at UT?"

"Sure. Is he still going with Estephanie?"

"Yeah, they're living together; I guess they're engaged. But they started doing event planning on the side, and it's kind of developed into a big deal. They were both majoring in education, but now, they're re-thinking that whole thing because the event planning is so lucrative."

"Especially in the Austin area. There's always something going on down there." Frau began gathering the dirty dishes to take to the sink, while Gino collected the condiments.

"Exactly. They started with quincenieras and bridal showers—you know, setting up the photo shoots at Lady Bird Johnson's wildflower center and Town Lake and finding venues for different occasions, but it's grown so big, they got one of those Margaritaville-type party buses to haul people from one venue to another. Then, last week, Juan mentioned that they had invested in a Hummer limo for the fancier affairs. Snob appeal, I guess. Who doesn't like being picked up in a nice limo? The guy they bought it from is military, so the Hummer was camo. I hope they haven't already painted it white. The camo would be a nice touch for our purposes." Gino started scrolling numbers on his cellphone.

"You're not kidding! That would be perfect! Atkins would really be impressed with that kind of service!"

"Yeah, so let me call Juan and make sure it's available; I'll ask him to hold off on painting it until we use it to pick Atkins up."

After speaking to Juan, Gino called Frau with an update: "I got him just in time before he painted the Hummer white and asked him if we could borrow it for a day or two. He didn't ask me any questions; he said just bring it back in one piece if at all possible. He's got some weddings lined up in a couple of months and wants to paint it as soon as we're through with it."

"Holy crap! Someone is really paving the way for us to get this done. It couldn't be any more perfect!" Frau rubbed her hands gleefully in anticipation.

"True. And he will have no problem letting me drive it. He's been trying to persuade me to pitch in with them, at least until I get an engineering job. And they're doing really well, so I'm considering it."

"I don't blame you. Event-planning is a very profitable enterprise right now. Proms, bachelor parties, tailgates—all sorts of occasions are getting professional help these days."

"Yeah, it's definitely working in our favor. I'll text Juan when you confirm the dates."

"Good deal, 'cause things are moving really fast."

"When is Pam coming over?"

As soon as Jackson sets up a time with Atkins, I'll alert her so she can get here to set up. She said she's ready to play."

"If I know Pam, she's going to really toy with him, just for the hell of it." Gino looked eager to see Pam in action.

"You got that right," Frau snorted.

They didn't have to wait for long. Jackson called with an update.

"Atkins wants to parley. How soon can Pam get to your house?"

"Probably thirty minutes. She just lives in Irving." Frau glanced at Gino, giving him a thumbs-up.

"Okay. Tell her she's got two hours before we Skype. That gives her time to get camera-ready. I mean, I know you ladies like to take your time getting ready for big events."

"Jackson, I am shocked! So condescending! But you're right. She'll want time to de-brief and paint the old barn."

Quickly, she texted Pam: "Can you be at my house in two hours?"

Pam responded, "Of course. I'm on my way."

"Well," Frau chuckled. "Let the games begin."

13

At 4:00 PM, Pam's truck pulled into Frau's driveway. She emerged from the truck looking glamorous. She'd blown her hair out big 'cause big Texas hair is what outsiders expect. Her make-up was impeccable, toned-down and classy, unlike the dark cherry lipstick that she preferred. And the piece de resistance—a low-cut blouse barely covering her assets—her "breast friends," as she called them. With men, Pam always knew how to turn-up the heat.

When Frau opened the door, she exclaimed, "Wow! You look amazing!"

"I know, right?" Pam giggled. "You know me. I want to do this right."

"Well, if Atkins isn't salivating at a chance to meet this—in all your gloriousness—there's something wrong with him."

"So when do I go on?"

"At 5:15, so you've got an hour and fifteen minutes to go over anything or ask questions. Jackson and Gino are here setting up the scene. Jackson has a Power Point that you can use, or he can do that part, if you'd prefer."

"No, girl. I can do that. I may be old-school, but when it comes to technology, I stay current."

"Perfect. Let's go to the den and see what they've got." She led the way to a room at the back of the house.

When they entered the room, Frau was surprised to see how they had set the stage. It looked so authentic, she almost forgot it was in her house. They had effectively created a hunting lodge, complete with faux animal heads, a fireplace with a low fire crackling since it was still Fall and not cold enough for an inferno, gun racks and a locked gun cabinet.

"Where did you get all this stuff?" Frau asked after she'd taken it all in. "This looks like a lodge Hemingway would have stayed in."

"Yeah, thanks. You remember my sister's brother-in-law, James, the actor?" Jackson reached up to straighten a picture on the wall.

"Of course, one of the Greer kids. I taught him English in the eleventh grade."

"Right. Well, I called him, thinking he likely had connections with prop people, and he hooked me up. His theater company has a big warehouse filled with all kinds of props, and they let me borrow whatever I needed. Do you think it's too much? I can tone it down. Too little? I've got more stuff out in the car."

"No, really, it's perfect, down to those liquor bottles and brandy decanters. It looks like an old movie set, as if some hunters will come walking through the door after the day's shoot and pour themselves drinks." Frau was visibly impressed, surveying their work slowly, as if she were looking at magnificent scenery.

"Well, it helped that you haven't updated this room. It still has wood paneling from the sixties, I would guess."

"You are not wrong. I think that's exactly right. So for once, my reluctance to update has paid off."

"Definitely," Jackson said with a smile. "Now, if only Pam is as convincing."

"Don't worry. Wait until you see her. It's a role she was born to play."

As if on cue, Pam walked in and struck a pose. "What do you think, Big Guy?"

"Man, you are smokin' hot, Ms. Pam. I mean, you clean up real good."

"Oh, ye of little faith. Did you have any doubts?"

"No, Frau pretty much told me you'd bring it." Jackson whistled appreciatively.

Gino turned around and said, "Wow, Pam, you look fan-tastic!"

"Thank you, boys. It's nice to see that my work has paid off. Now, tell me. Is there anything I need to know? I want this to go off without a hitch."

"Let's take a look at this Power Point. You can use it— or not—depending on how things are going."

Jackson clicked on "Lone Star Guided Hunts," and a beautiful scene depicting a Texas landscape at sunrise appeared. Subtle Vivaldi music played as the sun rose, revealing cacti in a lush semi-desert setting.

"Oh, that's beautiful!" Pam exclaimed.

"Yep. Straight out of Hill Country archival photos," Jackson explained.

The next frame showed a fairly elaborate hunting lodge with a horse-filled corral and ATV's in the background. It was clear that there would be no true "roughing it" here. The caption claimed, "Guided hunting tours throughout the day; first-class relaxation and amenities at night. OR . . . " The next frame appeared, showing a rustic cabin in a more austere setting with the caption, "Experience the frontier on your own or with small groups. Guides assist with tracking animals in their natural habitat." More beautiful pictures of the terrain appeared, interspersed with photos of hunters and their game.

Followed by that were price lists.

"One-day introductory tour for the novice: $5,000. Learn the ropes. Tour the Hill Country."

"Hunters' Surprise, basic package . . . $10,000 for two days of hunting, accompanied by a guide. No guarantees. The outcome depends entirely on the individual's prowess and expertise. Overnight in four-person tents; reach hunting areas on horseback."

"Premium Package—the Rugged Cowboy Experience—$25,000: Three days of stalking, using ATV's and horseback for rugged areas. Guaranteed outcome based on hunter's preference. Overnight in cabins with modest amenities. Chuck wagon barbeques each evening."

"The Ultimate Experience—$35,000: Pre-arranged prey delivery, based on hunter's choice of big game cats, rhinos, elephants, zebra, other exotic game. Three days of full-time, professional hunting assistants, photo shoots, travel via Hummer to hunting sites. Overnight in a first-class hunting lodge with ensuite rooms and open bar."

"Okay, I get it. I'm pitching the 'Rugged Package,' right?" Pam asked.

"Actually, it doesn't matter. Sell him on anything. Offer him the moon. Just get him here. 'Cause once he gets in that Hummer, he's going straight to the staging area – no amenities required, " Frau said. "Gino, what have you got?"

"I rigged a backpack filled with water and a hidden tracking device; if he ditches the backpack, I'm also providing him with a camouflage vest containing power bars and another tracking device. We've got to keep up with him."

"Weapons?"

"He's getting a basic bow, nothing fancy. If he's such a great bow-hunter, I believe he should be able to put it to good use."

"Agreed. Pam, one last thing. In setting this up, Jackson has been referring to you as 'Clarice.' Is that all right? It won't throw you off?"

"No, that's kind of sexy. I like it. But why did you pick 'Clarice'?" she asked Jackson.

"It's that news anchor on Channel Four. I think she's gorgeous; I've always kind of had a crush on her. And by the way, Atkins knows me as 'Casey Harold'. Don't let it throw you if it comes up."

"Good to know." She grimaced slightly, hoping she wouldn't forget anything. She hated last-minute instructions.

"Hey, we're approaching five-fifteen. Anything else?"

"I don't think so. I'm ready to rock-and-roll." Pam blew Gino a kiss, adjusted her low-cut blouse for maximum viewing, flipped her big, waist-length hair over her shoulder, then pouted slightly.

Jackson counted down, " . . . three, two one . . . " and pointed at Pam.

Pam looked directly at the camera as if coolly assessing the person on the other end and said seductively, "So, Mr. Atkins, we meet at last."

"Yes, Clarice, is it? I'm pleased to meet you."

"The pleasure is all mine," Pam retorted without cracking a smile. "Mr. Harold has been updating me on your progress and sent me to seal the deal."

"Well, of course, I haven't made a decision yet," he replied. "I'm still considering my options."

"Precisely. Your options are my area of expertise. What will it take for us to finalize this deal?" She uncrossed and recrossed her legs. Atkins watched intently.

After a slight hesitation, he said, "I'm sure you know my concern. At this moment, I'm trying to stay out of the spotlight. No publicity. I want to do this completely anonymously."

"Huh," she scoffed. "Do you think you are the first client to request that? We have politicians and celebrities coming in for a weekend shoot all the time. They don't want their constituents or audiences to know that they participate in such a controversial pastime. We pride ourselves on discretion. Have you heard of anyone using our services?"

"Actually, no."

"That's because we work to protect our clients. Believe me, we have some well-known clients who love to hunt but don't want anyone knowing that. It might cost them some votes or some Nielsen ratings."

"That takes care of that concern. Another problem is, I want to drive there and avoid being seen at the Austin airport, but Mr. Harold has been trying to convince me otherwise."

Pam smiled broadly and said, "Mr. Atkins, you will have to trust me on this. Our little regional airport gets a lot of semi-famous people and politicians coming through all of the time. You know Sandra Bullock and Matthew McConaughey have homes in the area and, of course, there's Willie Nelson. So people in Austin are used to seeing celebrities. George W. drops in from time to time; after all, Austin is the state capitol. If there are any paparazzi around, they'll be looking for them. But more to the point, we are two days away from staging a hunting expedition, and I'd like for you to be in it, so the only way you're going to make it is if you fly. I will personally pick you up at the airport and run interference for you. Don't worry your pretty head about it. Your safety and comfort are my chief concern." Again she smiled and lowered her eyelids. "I am at your service."

"Hmmm, interesting," Atkins said, smiling back. "Will you be going on the hunting expedition, too? It might help the time pass to have a lovely lady on the trip."

"Whatever you want, Mr. Atkins. I am entirely at your disposal." Her eyelashes fluttered languidly.

"All right, then. I can make arrangements to fly in tomorrow. I'll email Mr. Harold the flight info once I have everything arranged. You'll pick me up?"

"Of course. I am a cowgirl at heart, and I can't wait to give you the cowboy experience." She smiled and flipped her hair.

"Which package do you recommend?"

"The premium package features the 'rugged cowboy experience.' I like it rough."

"Do you now? Because you look like a high maintenance diva who prefers luxury hotels with all the amenities."

"Appearances can be deceiving, Cowboy. So, do we have a deal?"

"Absolutely. I can't wait. This is proving to be more exciting than I originally thought, thanks to you. I'll see you tomorrow, Clarice. I'll bring a cashier's check. You and I are going to have some fun together; I can just tell. Yippee-kai-yay!"

As the computer screen went blank, Pam muttered, "Yippee-kai-yay my sweet ass, mother-fucker. I ain't your whore, and we aren't going anywhere together, 'cause you're going straight to hell. How'd I do, kids?" she asked, confident in their response.

"Oh, you played him. He just doesn't have a clue," Frau said laughing.

"That joker is in for a rude awakening if he thinks I'm going to play footsie with him. He's never going to lay a finger on my fine ass! Dream on, sucker!"

"Oh, Pam," Jackson interjected. "You really, really brought it! It was amazing to watch you work your magic! I bow to the master," as he bent over several times from the waist to pay homage to her.

Gino hugged her and said, "You are a remarkable woman, Miss Pam. I've never seen anyone weave a spell like you did. What a tease!"

"No," Pam replied. "I am, pure and simple, an überbitch. I've spent years perfecting my technique. I haven't met the man yet who can resist my charm. You boys should be taking notes so you can avoid being victimized yourselves. People who know and love me appreciate my finer qualities; I don't give a shit about the others. That's my real claim to fame; I am unassailable!"

"And humble," Gino said. "This is a day I won't forget. I got to see the master at work!"

"Now, I'm going to have to go home and take a hot shower to get the 'yuck' off of me. That sleazy weasel has left me feeling dirty—and not in a good way."

Suddenly, Pam walked briskly to Frau, grabbed her by the shoulders and said, "Frau, let me do it. Let me pick Atkins up at the airport. I've got a .45 that's not traceable. Please, let me do it as a favor. I'll pick him up, drive him to the boonies, and he'll just disappear."

Mildly shocked but not surprised, Frau said, "Pam, you know I don't condone killing. I do wish I could indulge you, but I have principles. And that kind of talk might give Jackson a heart attack."

"You are certainly right about that, Frau. Frankly, Pam, I am shocked that you would so casually offer to kill him. I get it, but we are not supposed to be in the killing business. Or are we?" He looked directly at Frau.

"Oh, get off your moral high horse, Jackson. You know me better than that. We're here to teach him a lesson—a hard lesson, for sure, but murder is not on our agenda."

"Well, I have never felt so icky," Pam declared, shuddering. "Honestly, if anyone ever deserved to be put out of his misery, it's Jeff Atkins." As she walked out the door, Pam called over her shoulder, "Call me if you change your mind. I'm ready and willing." As she closed the front door, she winked at Gino.

"Thanks, Pam! Great job!" Frau chuckled. "Do you think she was serious?"

Gino said, "I believe she would murder him in his sleep, put him in a wood chipper, and feed the remnants to the coyotes. She's icy that way. I like her so much." He watched as she climbed into her pick-up and drove quickly away, kicking up gravel.

14

The three hour drive to Austin was uncharacteristically quiet, except for an occasional perfunctory question, followed by a monosyllabic response.

"Did you remember to call Mo?"

"Yep."

"Have you got the backpack?"

"Yeah."

"Did you tell your mother you were leaving?"

"Nope."

Everyone was lost in thought riddled with anxiety. Or was it anticipation?

Even Jackson was silent. Frau suspected he was secretly "flopping" in the backseat. Gino was at the wheel. She was riding shotgun. After Pam left, everyone scrambled to get their supplies loaded into Gino's truck. He made a quick trip to the corner station to fill the gas tank, called Juan to let him know they were on their way and took a shower. He figured it might be a while before he got another opportunity. Of the three, he believed he would be playing the biggest role in Austin.

Now, as they reached Austin's outskirts, Gino exited at 52nd St. on the north side and headed straight to Juan and Estephanie's business. They had an office near the highway, and the limo was parked in the back lot. After they dispensed with greetings and hugs, they hammered out the details.

"How long will you need the limo?" Juan asked.

"Oh, you'll have it back by morning," Frau promised. "We just need it long enough to pick up a guy from the airport and deposit him at his destination which is just a little southwest of here."

"Still don't want to tell me what's going on?" Juan asked, knowing that he wouldn't get a response.

"No, this is one of those deals where, the less you know, the better it is for you." Frau smiled at Estephanie.

"Uh huh," Juan nodded in mock agreement.

"Trust me on this," she said.

"Oh, don't worry. I trust you completely," he said and gave her a side-arm hug. "The tank is filled. It's been detailed. There's no rain in the forecast. Everything should be fine. Here are the keys." He handed the ring to Gino.

"Okay, Gino, we're heading on down to the ranch to set up. You got the flight information and the directions?" Frau was checking her notes for last-minute instructions.

"Oh, yeah. I'm ready. Do you want to go over the checklist again?"

"No need. We've got everything in the truck. You just need to pick up our stooge and deliver him to us."

"Yeah. The flight arrives in forty-five minutes. It's probably another thirty minutes to pick up the baggage and forty-five more to the site, depending on traffic."

Glancing at his watch, Gino pulled at the collar of his shirt, futilely trying to loosen it.

"Okay. We'll expect you around 3:00 PM then," she said.

"Frau? Just one question."

"Yeah?"

"Do I really have to wear this ridiculous outfit? I feel like a fool."

"Gino, you're driving a limo. Do you seriously think it would look normal for you to wear jeans and a t-shirt? You've got to make it look authentic." Frau stood with her hands on her hips, looking somewhat exasperated.

"Yeah, I suppose. But I feel degraded – you know, like those people who put clothes on their dogs. It's humiliating."

"You'll get over it," she laughed. "Remember how you want to be an actor? Here's your chance."

"Well, where's Scarlett Johansen then?" He tossed the keys to his truck to Jackson and watched as he and Frau got in the front seat.

"Bon Voyage! Bon Chance!" Gino waved as they left the parking area.

"Same to you!" they said in unison.

Suddenly, Gino felt all alone. He knew the ball was in his court. If he made one tiny misstep, it would be over in a second.

"Well, Juan, I'm gonna head on over to the airport and get situated. I don't want to be driving around looking for a place to park this big-ass monstrosity."

"No shit, man. Whatever ya'll are up to, Buena suerta!" He shook Gino's hand and stepped back so he could get in the limo. "Hey, who's bringing the car back?"

"Probably Jackson. I'll text you."

"Okay." Juan stepped away.

Gino drove slowly out of the lot, a little nervous at the responsibility that he now bore, but exhilarated at the same time.

The drive to the airport took ten minutes. Gino struggled with how to greet Atkins. Be aloof? Professionally detached? Friendly? *How the hell is a limo driver supposed to act?* He settled on reserved but polite—and accommodating: "Can I help you with your bags, sir?" *God, he hoped the plane was on time. Waiting is nerve-wracking.*

He turned the air-conditioning on high, trying to stay cool in the ridiculous limo driver uniform. He didn't want to appear nervous—or sweaty. *Look the guy in the eye, firm handshake, keep it cool. Oh, crap. How did I let Frau talk me into this? I could be at home watching a movie, eating a burger. Not this bullshit.* Inside the terminal, he checked the arrival/departure board. *Good, his flight's on schedule. Less time to think. I just want to get going.*

Of course, he knew what Atkins looked like, between the media coverage and the Skype meeting, but he was still worried that he'd somehow overlook him. *I bet he'll be wearing a ball cap to try to disguise himself. He seemed a little paranoid about being noticed.*

Finally, he spotted Atkins despite the cap he wore. He was the only guy in the terminal who was constantly looking down, so obviously trying to avoid being noticed. It had the opposite effect. People were looking at him, trying to figure out who he was. Luckily, no one did. Gino approached him with a crisp, "Good afternoon, sir. Let me help you with that." He took Atkins' bag from his willing hands.

"How many additional bags do you have, sir?"

"Two," Atkins responded. "One has my personal effects; the other, my bow."

"Very well, sir. I can help with that." *Oh, shut up, you big dope! Of course, you'll help him! That's your job!"* Gino wondered how much real limo drivers make.

"Good flight?" he asked.

"Well, I'm here," Atkins smirked. "There was some turbulence, but I'm used to it. I travel a lot."

I'm sure you do, you asshole, Gino thought.

"Hey, where's my little friend Clarice? She was supposed to meet me here. She promised me a good time."

"Unfortunately, there was an unexpected emergency that she had to attend to. She asked me to assure you that she would check in with you later."

"That's good. I'm looking forward to meeting her in person. She's just the feisty kind of little lady that I like." Atkins' eyes gleamed.

"Yes, sir. Clarice is special to all of us."

Finally, the two bags showed up on the carousel.

"This way, sir," Gino said, shouldering the two bags and carry-on.

Atkins followed him, striding confidently.

Gino decided to engage in some idle chitchat to get a feel for Atkins' true nature.

"First trip to Austin, sir?"

"First trip to Texas."

"How do you like it so far?"

"Not impressed," Atkins said dismissively. "It looks like a whole lot of nothing."

We're not even out of the airport yet, Gino thought with some amusement. *Maybe he's pissed off that Clarice didn't show up.*

"Looking forward to the hunt?"

Sure, I always get a thrill once I have big game in my sights." Atkins seemed pleased at this turn in the conversation.

"The drive to the ranch is quite scenic. The Hill Country is really beautiful, especially this time of year."

"Scenery doesn't get me going. It's the thrill of the chase and knowing I'm in control."

"The Lone Star organization is first-rate. I'm sure you'll enjoy your experience."

"I'll be the judge of that. A lot of these outfits make great promises but fail to deliver. I hate to waste my money." Atkins was looking around to see if anybody noticed him. Gino thought he almost looked disappointed that no one recognized him. It occurred to him that he was probably relishing his notoriety. *What a jerk,* Gino concluded.

Gino stored Atkins' bags in the luggage compartment of the limo and watched carefully to see where he kept his cellphone. So far, it had not rung or beeped with a message; Gino wondered if he had turned it off during the flight and forgot to turn it back on.

After they pulled out of the airport parking lot and drove the short distance to merge with I-35 headed south, Gino glanced over to see Atkins texting. He was completely focused on his cellphone exchange. That was a relief to

Gino who had grown weary of their forced exchange. The weather was great; the traffic was flowing smoothly, and Gino was soon lost in thought about what lay ahead.

With Jackson behind the wheel of Gino's truck and Frau navigating, they arrived at Mo's ranch sooner than expected, where they were met by Mo's foreman, Hank Trent. Hank offered apologies from Mo who had left the day before to attend a political rally. "Before we head out, would you like something to eat or drink? I imagine you're kind of tired from the drive."

"Nothing for me, thanks," Frau said. "Jackson?"

"No, Frau, I'm good."

"All right. I guess we'll head out then. Just follow me. It's not far, but it's tricky because the roads are not well-marked. They're more like trails, actually."

"Mo mentioned that it was pretty rough."

"And, of course, there's no gas stations or anything, so did you all stop at Fuel City down the road?"

"Oh, yeah, we filled up, checked fluid levels, tire pressure – all that."

"Great. Let's roll."

The terrain was rugged without a doubt. There were ruts and potholes. The road was merely a meandering trail. Frau got a kick out of the jack rabbits and lizards she spotted along the way. She figured when it got dark, there would be plenty more critters, just not immediately visible. Anticipation was building, and her heart was racing.

"I hope we haven't forgotten anything," she remarked.

"Frau, you can relax. We went over our list so many times, I would be astonished if we forgot even the most insignificant thing. We got this. When the three of us put our heads together, it's a beautiful thing. Everything's in sync." His sonorous voice was very calming.

"I know. I'm just a worrier by nature."

"That's a good thing, actually. It forces you to focus."

"True." Frau grew silent, absorbed in the beauty of the surroundings.

She recalled growing up in Corpus Christi in the 50's when horned toads—colloquially referred to as "horny toads"—were in abundance. There were families of them everywhere, and she and her sisters loved playing with them. Now, they are critically endangered due to loss of habitat, the proliferation of deadly fire ants and development. *What a sad thing*, she thought. *People just ruin everything. Those horny toads used to be so cute—like little dragons—and so fun to watch. Now, it's against the law to even touch one—if you can find them. Tragic.* Thinking about the demise of the horned toads fueled Frau's passion to punish someone – in this case, Atkins.

Once they arrived at the site, they bid Hank "adieu" and hurriedly emptied the truck of the supplies. Gino had managed to wrangle two more drones from his racing buddies—not top of the line because they didn't want to part with those—but good enough for their endeavor. There were also cases of water, G2, and Red Bulls, energy bars and trail mix. Gino had packed the backpack and vest with the tracking devices and the bow that would be Atkins' only weapon in the field. They noticed a couple of outbuildings and decided the larger of the two would serve as their headquarters for the duration.

"We'll store everything in there for now until Gino gets here with Atkins. He's the only one who knows about the drones. And, Jackson, if you want to leave now, I understand. I don't want you doing anything unsavory or contrary to your values. You know that."

"Frau, I wouldn't be here if I didn't want to be. I've been doing a lot of soul-searching lately, and you know what I've concluded? 'God helps those who help themselves.' I don't think God will blame me for taking justice into my own hands since the earthly courts wouldn't do it. I'm not going to invoke His name or anything; I'm just here to support my friends."

"Okay, but you know . . . " she started before he interrupted her.

"I do."

As it approached 3:00 PM, Frau observed, "It's floppin' time." Jackson nodded in agreement.

They could see the dust stirred up by Hank Trent's truck as he made his second trip of the day to the site, followed by the camo-limo.

"Here they come," Jackson whispered, as if someone nearby were listening.

"Let's do this," she said, trying to sound confident. This time, Hank did not stop; he made a u-turn and waved a good-bye out the window.

Atkins had arrived at last.

In a quick aside to Jackson, Frau asked, "Did you remember to remove the plates on Gino's truck?"

"All secured, Frau."

Atkins emerged from the limo obviously confused – and not a little hostile. "What's going on here? What kind of bullshit is this?"

"Welcome, Mr. Atkins," Frau said politely. "We have been awaiting your arrival."

"This is not what I signed on for. First, Clarice fails to show, and now, I'm in the middle of nowhere with no lodging in sight."

"We understood you like it rough, Mr. Atkins. It doesn't get much rougher than this."

"Oh, so now, you're twisting my words? You know, I've got a helluva lawyer who will rip you to shreds. This is bait-and-switch, pure and simple, and it's illegal on a lot of levels."

"Bait-and-switch? What can you possibly mean? You signed up for the adventure of a lifetime, and we're about to give it to you."

"How so? This run-down encampment is hardly worth the $25,000 I paid for."

"Did you already get the check, Cobra?"

"Got it right here, Black Mamba." He waved the check back and forth.

"Good. You will be pleased to know, Mr. Atkins, that we are donating that money—anonymously, of course; we wouldn't want your big-game hunting friends to know you are making such a sizeable contribution to a game conservation group in Namibia. But you'll have the satisfaction of knowing that you're helping save big game from people like yourself."

"People like me? What's that supposed to mean?" He snarled.

"Oh, you know, people with no conscience, no scruples, no integrity, people who kill animals for fun."

"I kill animals for sport—for the challenge."

"So you can have a nice big taxidermied head hanging on your den wall for your hunting buddies to see! Those animals would look so much better roaming in their native habitat than frozen on your wall."

"That's just like you tree-hugging, animal-loving hypocrites—what I do supports the wildlife; it weeds out the sickly, elderly animals that are going to die anyway. You sicken me."

"Careful, Atkins," Jackson advised.

"So . . . The Unicorn was sickly and elderly? I don't think so. From what I've heard, he was still the patriarch of a vibrant herd and still producing viable offspring."

"Say what you will. Everything I did was done according to the law. I was not indicted. The government is pursuing the guides; they misled me."

"A veteran hunter like you? Hard to believe. You may have wanted to be misled so you could blame your crime on others. Very convenient. But now it's time to face the proverbial music."

"So what's your plan? To bore me to death? 'Cause that's what you're doing." He put his hand to his mouth as if feigning a yawn.

"No, actually, we have something quite challenging for you. I personally think you'll like it. We're going to give you the opportunity to show what a really great hunter you are."

"Let's hear it, Miss Whoever-you-are."

"Just call me Black Mamba. Your driver is Cobra, and the third part of our group is Viper."

"More nonsense. I guess that's to be expected from a bunch of misfits."

"I told you to tread lightly, Atkins," Jackson warned.

"It'll be a cold day in hell when I take orders from a punk-ass kid."

"All right, I warned you." Jackson made a quick grab, putting Atkins in a chokehold.

Atkins elbowed Jackson and broke away, as Frau said, "Cobra . . ." Jackson tackled Atkins, throwing him to the ground and saying, "Don't worry, Mamba. I got this," and slammed Atkins' face in the dirt. With Atkins struggling to escape Jackson's tight grasp, Jackson drove his knee into Atkins' back and punched him as hard as he could in mid-torso. Throughout the melee, Frau could hear Jackson say, "Punk-ass kid? I got your punk-ass. Now whatcha gonna do about it? I tried to be reasonable, and you just wouldn't listen. This could have been so easy, but you wanted to make it difficult. I was brought here to be the voice of reason, but there's no reasoning with idiots like you!" Jackson pounded Atkins so brutally that, finally, Gino pulled him off. Frau promptly rolled Atkins over to make sure he was still conscious.

Gasping and spitting out dirt, Atkins said, "This isn't over, you ignorant bastard. You're gonna pay big-time. If you ever get out of jail, I'm gonna make your life miserable!"

"You first," Jackson snorted. "The only reason—the only freakin' reason you aren't already dead is because I blocked Clarice from using her untraceable pistol on you! That's right! Clarice wanted to put you out of your misery. Our mission is to teach your dumb-ass a lesson—not kill you. But now, I'm sorry I didn't listen to her. You are vermin and need to be exterminated!"

Atkins' eyes grew wide with terror as Jackson continued to rant. There was no stopping him. Once Frau interrupted him, saying, "Viper, I had no idea you had it in you. You went from GQ to ghetto in five seconds flat."

Jackson rose to his full 6'2" and looked fierce. "He's just lucky to be alive. No more Mr. Nice Guy! Just give me a chance. I'm going to do everything in my power to thwart his endeavors!"

"Calm down, Viper," Gino prevailed. "This is getting us nowhere. We need to proceed with the plan."

"I know you're right, but my instinct right now is just to eradicate him," he said, snarling at Atkins who looked very subdued.

"All right, Mr. Atkins, here's the deal," Frau spoke through clenched teeth. "You're here to show us what a great hunter you are. We're going to leave you here over the weekend to contend with the weather and the wildlife with minimal equipment and no guide. It's all on you. We're challenging you to demonstrate your skill without all the expensive equipment and amenities that you've grown accustomed to in your rarefied world. You have become complacent and over-confident. We bet you lose."

Despite his battered condition, Atkins arrogantly responded, "Since I have no choice, I accept your challenge. I will show you how skilled I am at survival and, at the end of the weekend, I'm going straight to the cops and have you arrested. You will not likely see the light of day for many years once they get through charging you with kidnapping, extortion, terroristic threats, battery and whatever else I can think of."

"Au contraire, mon frère. Kidnapping? You came here of your own volition. Extortion? I already explained we aren't touching that money. Battery? Well, maybe, but two witnesses saw you attack first. You kind of have nothing, really. This is a gentleman's challenge, nothing more," Frau concluded politely.

"One way or the other, you'll pay for this. People can't get away with crimes."

"And that's exactly our point. Since Namibia declined to indict, we've taken up the mantle of justice to insure that The Unicorn did not die in vain. So here's what we've got: a backpack with water and energy bars, and a hunter's vest loaded with necessities—like a snake-bite kit and a compass. I hope you know how to use it because there's no GPS here. This is a wilderness area. There's no telling what you'll encounter in the next forty-eight hours. That's when we'll pick you up. From 5:00 PM on Friday to 5:00 PM on Sunday, you're on your own to battle the elements and whatever critters you encounter. Oh, by the way, Cobra. Did you get his cellphone?"

"Yeah, I picked it up when it flew out of his pocket in the scuffle."

"Can I have my luggage? I need my bow," Atkins demanded.

"Um, no. actually, we have a bow for you. Cobra, get that bow for Mr. Atkins."

When he returned, Atkins snorted derisively. "That thing? Are you fucking kidding me? That thing is worthless, a child's toy. My bow is professional; it cost thousands."

"Nevertheless, this is the bow you're getting. I can't have you out there killing wildlife indiscriminately with a weapon that gives you an unfair advantage, now, can I?"

"But I can't survive with this piddly-ass thing. It's a joke!"

"Tell it to The Unicorn. This is much more of a chance than you gave him – or any of the other magnificent animals that you've slaughtered. Now, be a good boy and take your whippin' like a man."

"You got me fucked up, bitch. I will come out on top, you'll see." Spittle flew from his lips as he enunciated each syllable.

"Atkins, one more word, and I'll . . ." Jackson thundered.

"Water off a duck's back, Jack. This fool doesn't validate me. He's the most despicable, worthless, heartless, soul-less individual I have ever met. Watching him lose this match will be a pleasure. I hope you learn your lesson, Mr. Atkins, but I have a feeling you won't. I believe you are one of those sociopathic murderers who are unable to feel guilt or sorrow or compassion. You are trash and a blight on humanity. Let's go, boys."

Gino handed the vest and backpack to Atkins and laid the bow on the ground in front of him. He thought about saying, "Good luck," when he turned to leave, but decided he didn't really mean it, so he said nothing.

As they got in the truck to drive a short distance away, Frau thought how forlorn Atkins looked, standing there watching them leave. Sensing her weakening resolve, Jackson leaned in and whispered, "No mercy, Frau. He didn't give any to The Unicorn."

"No, not a drop," she spat out. *He deserves it*, she thought and then turned to the task that lay ahead.

"You got everything ready with the drones, Gino?"

"It won't take long to get them ready. I made sure the tracking devices are working before we left."

"I still wish I had Pam's gun," Jackson added. Gino and Frau just looked at each other and smiled.

15

As Atkins watched them drive away, he berated himself for being so stupid. *I can't believe I got conned. I should have sensed something wasn't right.* He attributed the lapse to stress. *When will it stop? I can't go back and un-do what I've done. But this? This is just insane! What a dope I am. I'd better quit wallowing in self-pity and get busy.* If he felt any regret, he wasn't going to let them know. Atkins was no dummy. He grew up hunting with his father and uncles. The weeks leading up to the first day of hunting season were filled with excitement. Preparing the equipment, cleaning the rifles, buying ammunition, getting the proper licenses—it was in his blood.

First and foremost, he knew he would have to keep a level head. It was pointless to panic. Assess the situation. Determine the best course. Execute the plan. Simple.

Atkins' big problem was not being familiar with the environment. Whenever he went to a new place to hunt, he relied on his guides to make arrangements, trouble-shoot, and insure his safety. Here, he had no one to advise him.

The lack of supplies was also troubling. *I don't know how long this stuff is going to last, so I'd better be frugal in the beginning. Friday to Sunday is only 48 hours. I'll have to make it*

*work so I can show those sanctimonious pricks that they're
messing with the wrong guy.*

Surveying the terrain for a strategic place to spend the
night yielded few prospects. The Hill Country has sparse
vegetation, scrawny mesquite trees not conducive as a safe
place to remain above any foraging critters, and lots of
gullies that no doubt harbor bothersome nocturnal animals.
He wasn't looking forward to dealing with them. The
coyotes might be a nuisance, but they're wary of humans.
Cougars, on the other hand, might present a challenge.

He was also a little concerned about the insects,
especially the scorpions. Where he came from, there were
no scorpions—too cold—but he had seen his share of
deadly scorpions on some of his exotic expeditions. They'll
crawl right into the sleeping bag with you. As long as
you're immobile, you're safe. But as soon as you move,
they strike. He shuddered at the thought.

Of course, there are spiders, but he didn't expect to
have a problem with them. He knew that people's fear of
tarantulas is largely based on their size, but they are, for
the most part, harmless. At least, the ones in the northern
hemisphere are. So what does that leave? Snakes. Atkins
was terrified of snakes. Once, while hunting jaguar in the
Amazon Basin, as he crouched in a blind waiting for a
perfect shot, a bushmaster –a particularly deadly pit
viper—crawled onto his boot, unknown to him, and rested
there. It wasn't until his guide jumped up and yelled,
alerting his prey and scaring him out of range that he
realized his peril.

"Holy crap! What do I do?" He hissed at his guide.

"Don't move. Just freeze until I can get the stick," he
replied in a strangled voice as he sprinted toward the
backpacks.

Atkins stayed in a very uncomfortable squatting position for several minutes until the guide could return just in time to fling the snake away. By that time, Atkins was dripping in sweat, and it took him several minutes to regain his composure.

"Why didn't you shoot?" He yelled, stomping off through the underbrush.

"Did you want me to risk shooting you in the foot? There is no doctor for miles. I couldn't risk it!" The guide was resolutely unapologetic.

"Idiots! I'm surrounded by idiots!" Atkins thundered. "What do I pay you for? You're supposed to protect me. You're worthless!" His rant continued when he realized his opportunity for a trophy had evaporated like snow in the spring.

Although this was his first trip to Texas, Atkins knew that snakes are prevalent. In his current situation, he didn't expect to encounter water moccasins. There seemed to be little water in the area. But he knew that there were likely rattlesnakes and copperheads.

Surely, they won't be a problem at night, he assured himself. *They like lounging in the sun. If I avoid rocky crevices, I should be all right.* Still, he would be super-cautious. The thought of dying from a snakebite with no access to medical help did not appeal to him.

Shouldering his backpack, he got an energy bar from his vest pocket and set out, heading west, according to the sun's position. Darkness would come soon, and he wanted to find a reasonably secure vantage point for the night—no fumbling around in the dark.

Not far away, he could see vultures circling in their ritual death watch. *I wonder what they're after. Probably a rabbit or something.* As he got closer, he could see that it was too big to be a rabbit. *Let's see what they've found*, he thought, his curiosity mounting. *What is that thing? Too small for a deer.* Upon closer examination, he muttered, "Oh, wow. It's a young pig." When he rolled the carcass over, he knew by the number of maggots that it had been dead for at least a day. The stench of death had just attracted the vultures. And then he noticed something odd. At first, he thought a coyote had gotten the little guy, but coyotes usually rip a big chunk out of their victim's body. And that was not the case. This pig was intact.

A little glint of metal got his attention. *That looks like a bullet fragment. Who's been out here shooting?* He turned around, looking over his shoulder and squinting in the distance. *This could be a game-changer. If someone is out here hunting, I could very easily become a target myself. I'd better try to get to that outcropping and position myself to watch out for knuckleheads in the dark.* The irony of his having lured The Unicorn out of his sanctuary in the dark did not occur to him.

Unnerved by this new development, Atkins picked up his step so he could get to the rocky precipice and survey the perimeter before nightfall. Seeing nothing remarkable, he settled in for the night. Sitting on the rocky outpost, he drank some water, watched the sun set and hoped for an uneventful night.

Sleep did not come easily. Every time a twig snapped, he jumped up and looked around. Insects swarmed around him, seeking his body heat. He slapped at them and flicked the bigger ones away, knowing how easily insect bites can become infected. All of his senses were heightened. The swish of a bush stirred by a breeze made his hair stand on end. He was terrified of having to duel with a predator in the dark. Although the sky was clear and the moon was full, the light needed to defend himself against a big cat was insufficient. He could be ripped to shreds in voracious jaws. He shivered at the prospect.

As night wore on and the wildlife seemed to calm down, Atkins dozed off, only to be awakened by a curious armadillo flicking his long tongue on his salty arm. Not knowing what was tickling him, he shrieked like a girl and sprinted away like a champion. *Jesus Christ! What the hell was that thing? It felt like sandpaper scraping my skin!*

After that incident, there was no sleeping. He thought about his wife, his girlfriend, that slutty Clarice, his kids, his father. He remembered the first time his father took him bow hunting. Zeroing in on a big-eyed raccoon, he misfired. The arrow didn't kill the little guy, and he ran off into the bushes. Following, urged on by his father to "Be quick about it," Atkins caught up with the unfortunate creature trying to pull the arrow out of his chest.

"Finish him off!" his father had yelled, giving the boy a shove.

The panicky boy thereupon grabbed a nearby rock and bashed the poor thing to death.

"You idiot!" his father screamed. "How could you let such an easy shot get by you? You're a disgrace! And when is it ever okay to use rocks? Unbelievable!"

Embarrassed and angry, the boy vowed to never let that happen again. Deep down, he knew that he had flinched before releasing the arrow, feeling a twinge of pity for the animal. *From now on*, he swore, *no mercy! It does them no good and actually makes things worse. A clean shot and a quick, merciful death—that's my goal.* And a cruel hunter was born.

Having survived the armadillo "attack," Atkins was hoping for a quick end to the night. Alas, it was not to be. No matter how hard he tried to reassure himself, or sleep, or think about pleasant things, he was distracted by the noises generated by unseen and unknown creatures of the night. *Who would have thought one night could be so long? Or that there would be so many startling sounds?*

Making him even more miserable was the cold. During the day, it had been a balmy 65 degrees, but after dark, the temperature quickly dropped twenty-five degrees. All he was wearing was the vest provided by Gino and his flannel shirt underneath. In the stillness, he sat shivering, trying to recall the sweltering heat of the savannah or the flush of warmth when drinking coffee from a thermos on an early-morning retreat. But Atkins' misery was relentless. Thinking of getting through the 48 hours and back home was little solace to him. The here-and-now demanded his full attention. There was no escape.

By Saturday morning, Atkins was stiff, cold and cranky, in addition to being bruised and sore from the day before. The energy bars and Red Bull were not sufficiently nutritious to fuel his foray into the unknown. He realized that he needed to get out of this God-forsaken place and back to the comforts of civilization. Once he got home, he was going to make Black Mamba and her cohorts pay for this insult. *How did they dare put him in this situation?* He surveyed the horizon in four directions, looking for a hint of the civilization he craved—telephone poles, planes, roads, anything. He was disappointed.

This federally protected land had no fiber optic network, no WiFi, no cell phone towers. Looking at the barren desert-like landscape, he realized that it was almost like being snow-blind. Everything was so similar, you fail to see any distinctions. Your eyes are blinded by the bright sunlight striking the crystals in the sand. The flashes of light made him wince as he attempted to shield his eyes from the glare.

Suddenly, Atkins became aware that there was a dull, humming sound coming from behind him. Imperceptible at first, it was growing louder, but rose only to the level of a murmur. *What is that?* Looking around, he spotted a small object coming at him and realized that a drone was approaching. *They're tracking me!* He knew little about drones and what they were capable of doing. *Do they have cameras? Is there a heat sensor? What distance limitations does it have? How is it fueled?* He had once had an opportunity to go to a drone race with his son but opted instead for a gun show. Now, he regretted the decision. *I wish I knew enough to turn the tables and use the drone to my advantage. If it got close enough, could I catch it? But then what? It doesn't have what I need. It's just another annoyance meant to drive me crazy. They're probably laughing at me. I may be going in circles.*

Using the compass, he believed, was not as effective as relying on the sun, as long as it was sunny. That could always change. He decided to quit obsessing about the drone and move on. The drone followed at a respectful distance.

What's that old saying? Not to decide is to decide? Atkins was convinced that eastward would be the most promising direction, so he set out in the direction of the sunrise. After pursuing that route for over an hour and seeing absolutely nothing in the landscape to give him hope, he decided to follow a gulley. His thought was that water attracts civilization. Occasionally, he would run across a small spot where water had pooled in defiance of the three-year Texas drought, of which Atkins knew nothing. Rushing to see what the water might have attracted, he recoiled to find a mass of water moccasins writhing in a slithery heap, savoring the tiny puddle, likely the last vestige of water in the area. *I'm not getting anywhere near that,* he shuddered, stumbling as he raced away from the deadly pool.

It was noon before Atkins decided to take a break. At first, his stride was long and deliberate, as if on a mission—which he was. A mission to survive 48 hours and get the hell out of Texas. But as the fruitless day wore on, his walk slowed, faltering from the burden of despair and frustration.

"Jesus, this is a God-awful place," he grumbled, as he struggled up yet another rocky hill. Spotting a rabbit, he considered killing it, but he had no matches, and despite his boy scout training, few prospects for starting a fire. He wasn't hungry enough yet to eat it raw. *That time may come,* he lamented, *but not yet.*

Sitting on a rock and sipping water to conserve as much as possible, he considered his options: 1) Keep going in the same direction; 2) Go back to his starting point and hope someone comes along; 3) Stay where he was and . . . *wait a minute! How stupid am I? I should follow the drone where it leads. It's clearly coming from their location. Where is that thing? Where's the last place I saw it?*

He realized that it had probably been a mile or so back since he last heard the thing humming behind him. *Where was it? Near that big patch of cactus I passed after I detoured from the gulley?*

Re-tracing his steps, he suddenly felt a surge of energy—the exhilaration of realizing he might have a chance now. Clearly, the key was to get back in range of that drone and find out how he could get the thing to reverse course so he could follow it back to those idiots who put him in this mess.

Meanwhile, at their command post, Gino realized immediately what Atkins was up to. As soon as he saw Atkins reverse course on the GPS device hidden in his vest, Gino told Frau, "He's going back after the drone." Unknown to Atkins, the drone's distance was limited. Once Atkins was out of range, the GPS picked up the trail. Gino monitored every move Atkins made—if not visually, then electronically. Atkins was unaware that he was following a circuitous route that kept him within a three mile range of his starting point.

Gino laughed. "Look, he's really picking up steam, thinking he'll find the drone and follow it home."

Indeed, as the Trifecta watched Atkins' blip on the monitor, they could see that he was nearly sprinting back to the cactus cluster where he last remembered hearing the drone. After a few minutes, however, his enthusiasm began to wane. The lack of sustenance was slowing him down, despite his best efforts and newfound sense of urgency.

Damn, I'm going to have to take a break. This ordeal is taking a toll on me. I guess I'm not as young as I thought. This is turning out to be a nightmare. Still, he was determined to get back to the drone.

Am I even going in the right direction? Maybe I should have used the compass after all, instead of relying on the sun, 'cause now I'm a little confused. I thought I was heading north when I followed the gulley, but then which way did I go? I was in such a rush to get away from those snakes, I guess I didn't notice. Think, man! Where was the sun then? Jeff Atkins the Great Hunter was beginning to unravel.

Hunger was gnawing at him, distracting him. *Those damn energy bars are worthless!* He raged to no one. After a fifteen-minute break, he resumed his mission, somewhat buoyed by the brief rest. *Come on, now,* he pleaded. *Help me out here. I really need to find those big succulents or whatever they are.*

What they were was tall, magnificent cacti of noble lineage. Common in the Hill Country, they provided food and refuge for the smallest denizens of the area. Their buttons were used in religious ceremonies to induce hypnotic effects and hallucinations. To the indigenous species, they were a god-send, storing water during the drought. To Atkins, they were just bread crumbs on the trail to civilization.

Atkins feared he was going in circles. With the sun directly overhead, it was hard to tell. And he couldn't find the compass. He realized he might have dropped it when he scrambled out of the gulley. *I can't catch a break!* He chided himself after frantically searching through the backpack.

Gino could only imagine what frantic measures Atkins was taking to get back to the drone-friendly area. The GPS showed him moving at a fairly quick clip for a short burst, then stopping for a time, then picking up the pace again. For a while, he veered off-course and seemed to be circling, but he eventually straightened himself out and maintained a direct approach.

"Frau, I don't know what his objective is, but he's re-tracing his steps for some reason," pointing to the blip on his laptop. "See, here's where he started, heading east, then north and now, west. I wish I could read his mind as well as trace his path. He's a wily one."

As Frau and Jackson leaned in to look at the screen, she snorted. "He's in for a little turbulence tonight. They're predicting a drastic drop in temperature and high winds. I don't think he's going to have much fun. He'd better start looking for a warm place. Maybe a cave. But he'd better be prepared to share it with some wild beast. And I don't think his bow will do much good."

"No, and all this walking and back-tracking has to be taking a toll on him. He's used to being transported and not doing much stalking. I'm guessing he's pretty beat. The Unicorn would be proud." Gino smiled.

16

During the lulls in Atkins' trek, Frau indulged herself in fantasies about the hell she hoped he was experiencing. When she was a child, she often went with her father and little sister to the Saturday movies on the Navy base. For a dime apiece, they could see a cartoon, an episode in the Buck Rogers series, and a feature-length picture, usually a Western. Some of the movies featured someone being tied up, covered in molasses or some sweet, sticky substance, and left on an ant mound to die a horrifying, slow death. She wished Atkins would suffer something excruciating like that.

Or there was the guy her niece told her about who was stomping around his property north of Dallas when he realized his gait had become uneven. Stopping to see what was causing the limp, he saw a squished spider so big, its body covered the heel of his boot. He casually flicked it off while Frau's niece shrieked in horror. The idea that spiders, insects and lizards, left to their own devices in rural areas, could reach such Brobdingnagian proportions, intrigued Frau. Maybe there's a gigantic spider waiting for Atkins in the boonies—like those enormous spiders in Harry Potter. She relished the thought. Nothing was too heinous for Atkins. He owed nature a huge debt, and nature just might exact her revenge.

She was startled from her reverie by Gino, who was calling, "Frau? Frau, come see this." He was pointing at an image on his laptop. Atkins had been chasing the drone, not paying attention, and had stepped into a hole. It wasn't particularly deep, but it jolted him and threw him off-balance. Now it appeared that his ankle had sustained an injury of some sort. Whether it was sprained or fractured was unclear, but it was definitely causing him problems. At the moment, he was rubbing his ankle, trying to assess the damage.

"Well," Frau observed, leaning in to get a better view, "Our boy is in a helluva mess now. If he can't walk, he's going to be pretty vulnerable. Are the vultures circling?"

"Not yet," Gino replied, trying to triangulate his exact location. "He's a good ways out there. I mean, I could take one of the ATVs in the shed and go pick him up."

"No," Frau said after consideration. "I think he needs to suffer a while. No mercy, remember?"

Gino sighed. He found himself pitying Atkins just a little in his current predicament. But the whole point of the exercise was to see how Atkins responded to the challenges of the wilderness.

He could see that Atkins was tearing off the sleeve of his shirt to create an Ace-type bandage to wrap around his ankle. It certainly didn't appear to be broken; it was probably sprained. But even that was going to be a big handicap.

Atkins was definitely having a rough time. As he wrapped his ankle, he was barely aware of the drone's presence. He was focused on relieving his pain so he could somehow hobble to a safer place. Right now, he was out in the open. And damn, he was hungry! *What am I going to do about that?* he wondered. There were plenty of little lizards scampering around, but he wasn't desperate enough to eat a lizard—yet. Instead, he hoped to spot a rabbit, maybe a bird. He could put his bow to use, but he'd still have to eat his kill raw, and that was revolting to him. He never even ate his steaks rare; it was always medium to well-done. Still, raw rabbit was starting to sound pretty good. *But where are the little beasts?* He realized he hadn't seen one since morning, but maybe as it gets closer to evening, they'll be out again.

In the meantime, his ankle was throbbing. Noticing the drone hovering in the distance, he wondered if he could hop enough to follow it. Crawling was out of the question. Staying put was also untenable. If only he could find a sturdy branch to use as a crutch. The straggly mesquite trees yielded nothing substantial enough to support him. Maybe he could lean a little on his bow—not too much. *I don't want to risk breaking it. I may need it before my time is up.*

He sat on a rock for awhile, contemplating his options. *I have no one to blame for this mess but myself,* he thought bitterly. *And that crazy woman and her minions. Is it possible that they will see my dilemma and come to my aid? I doubt it.* He resigned himself to finding a solution on his own. *It's me against the environment. Isn't that what she said? Well, I'm going to have to out-think them if I'm going to succeed.*

While Atkins pondered his fate, Gino was glued to the monitor at the command post when Jackson and Frau returned from dropping off the limo.

"What did we miss? The traffic was beastly," Frau said while hauling Jack-in-the-Box bags in from Gino's truck.

"Atkins is still favoring his ankle," Gino swung the monitor in their direction.

"Oh, wow, that does complicate things. I hope it's not broken. Oops, sorry. I know. No mercy." Jackson looked only slightly apologetic.

"No one with a heart could watch him without a little pity, no matter how reprehensible he is, so don't feel bad," Frau reassured him, patting him gently on the shoulder.

"Yeah," Jackson said unconvincingly.

"Maybe he'll be wise enough to find a safe place for the night. With his limited mobility, he would be smart to start looking now. There's not a whole lot of options out there. It's fairly flat except for that gulley area. I would avoid that because the animals will show up at night seeking water and snacks."

While Gino had never been to this particular area before, in his five years at U.T., he had been on excursions and retreats around Austin and was familiar with the terrain. "Again, I can go in after him if that's what you want to do. What do you think, Jackson?" Gino was totally focused on Atkins' predicament.

"I say, give him more time to ponder his sins or shortcomings or whatever you want to call it. This is supposed to be a learning process. If we go in at the slightest mishap, what's the lesson? That he will always manage to escape justice?"

Frau brushed a pesky fly away as she bit into a bean-and-cheese burrito and said, "Let's wait a while. If he can get to a spot where he's sheltered for the night, I think the experience will be forever seared into his pea-brain."

"Right," Gino said between bites of hash browns. "It's too soon. As long as we have him under surveillance, I can go in at any time, so there's no rush."

While they were enjoying their meal, Atkins was struggling across the uneven terrain using his bow as an aid. "Damn, this is rough ground," he muttered, as he looked over his shoulder to reassure himself that the drone was still tracking him. He was confident that, as vengeance-driven as Frau and her team were, they would not let him die out there. *The consequences for them would be severe if I were to die.* He hoped they weren't completely cold-blooded. *I wonder if anyone is looking for me or if my wife is wondering why I haven't called?* Of course, the answer was "no"; he had told her that he was going on a hunting excursion which meant that he would be incommunicado for a few days. *It's only been 24 hours—no reason for her to be alarmed.*

As he slowly, painfully maneuvered over a rise on his trek, he came to another gulley where water had pooled. Despite the drought, Austin sat atop an extensive aquifer system, and occasional pockets of water from underground springs would pop up. This spring had created a virtual oasis in the desert with lush foliage in abundance compared to the rest of the area.

At least I can rest here awhile. Atkins surveyed the landscape. *If I can find a high spot or a recess in the rocks, I should be all right.* After walking and hopping for what seemed an eternity, he finally found an outcropping that looked promising. *It gives me a good vantage point*, he thought, wincing as he slipped on some crumbly rocks. *If I get lucky, a rabbit will come by. I'm really hungry.* By this time, he was ready to overlook his aversion to raw meat.

Once he had positioned himself and felt safe enough to relax for a while, Atkins unintentionally dozed off. He was startled by a scrambling in the underbrush to his left. Thinking it was a juicy rabbit, he grabbed his bow to stand up, reached into the backpack for his arrows and poised himself to shoot the hapless little bunny. He was already imagining a tasty repast. Taking aim, he inched forward, but misjudging his balance, he lost his footing and started skidding down an incline. The pain shooting through his ankle was sharp, causing him to shift his weight to the left. Suddenly, he was in full sliding mode, completely out of control. "Shit!" he yelled. "Son-of-a-bitch!" He could not regain his footing; his hands were clutching at sprigs of undergrowth which broke under his weight. "Holy crap!" he yelled as he continued to slide straight into a thorny bush.

The commotion he created on his descent alarmed the little critters that were hiding in the bushes. Rabbits scampered away. Birds in the vicinity took flight. The only resident who didn't escape in time lay right in Atkins' path. Too late, he realized he was skidding straight into a skunk! The black and white coloring was unmistakable. Even if he'd had time to think, he would not have been able to change course. It was set. All he could do was hope the skunk would get out of his way. Unfortunately, it didn't happen. The only recourse the skunk had was to prepare to fire at the intruder. He unleashed his full arsenal of special skunk scent right into Atkins' face. "Oh, my God!" Atkins exclaimed, trying to shield himself from the onslaught, to no avail. The damage was done.

At Trifecta headquarters, Gino, who was tracking Atkins' every move via the drone, suddenly hollered, "Frau, come quick! You won't believe this!" Frau and Jackson rushed to see what had happened.

"Look, Atkins has been skunked! Oh, my God! This is hysterical! Look at him! He's dripping with skunk perfume!"

It took Frau a moment to process what was going on because Gino was laughing so hard, but when she realized what had occurred, she said, "Now, that's justice! The skunk got skunked! It's perfect! Now, he's really going to be miserable! There's not a can of tomato juice anywhere near him! He's going to have to just deal with it!"

"Tomato juice?" Jackson asked amid bursts of laughter. "What's that got to do with anything?"

"The conventional wisdom is, when someone's been shot with skunk juice, tomato juice will neutralize it. Dogs get sprayed all the time, and my groomer says that's how they get rid of the smell." Frau was intent on watching Atkins try to crawl away from the odiferous animal. "He's probably afraid the skunk is going to re-load, and he's scrambling away. But it doesn't regenerate that fast. He's got time to get away."

"Well, the skunk looks pissed." Gino howled with laughter. "This is the funniest thing I've ever seen. Wait 'til I show you the whole thing. When he started sliding, the look on his face was priceless! It was hilarious! Oh, man! It just kept getting better and better!" Tears were rolling down his cheeks from laughing so hard.

Drenched in Pepe le Pew cologne and aching from the punishment his ankle took in the slide, Atkins struggled to drag himself out of the gulley. The sky was already darkening, and he knew that before long, the water hole would attract numerous critters, some of which he wanted to avoid given his physical predicament.

"Jesus," he said aloud while clutching at branches to pull himself up. "This is unfucking believable. I can't stand this stench." He began to gag. While he had contemplated dunking himself in the water, he gave up the idea because he had no way of gauging its depth or of knowing if there were water moccasins hanging around. "God, I've got another twenty-four hours of this," he moaned. *If those assholes were going to help me, you'd think they'd have done it after all this.* It suddenly struck him that they might not help him after all, despite his earlier conviction that they were too compassionate to watch him suffer. *Oh, I am so screwed,* he thought dejectedly as he continued to claw his way to the top of the ridge.

By this time, Gino had recalled the drone on account of darkness and was relying solely on the tracking devices he'd planted on Atkins. "He hasn't moved much at all. I imagine it's slow going for him with his ankle in such bad shape. I wonder what that skunk scent will attract?"

"You should have paid better attention in Mr. Mac's AP Biology class," Jackson opined, while peering over Gino's shoulder at the monitor. "Then you'd know. Nothing. That scent is a repellent; it doesn't attract a darn thing."

"Yeah, you'd think, but he was more focused on reproduction and genetics. I don't remember a thing about wildlife aside from nomenclature and something about Darwin's Origin of Species. Scent glands were not in the curriculum." Gino never looked away from the monitor.

"It's a powerful unrelenting smell, that's for sure." Frau laughed as she unscrewed the top of a classic Coke. "He should be feeling really miserable right about now. I wouldn't want to be in his stinky shoes."

"Ready for me to go after him yet?" Gino asked again.

"In your truck?" She laughed at the thought of Gino putting the unfortunate Atkins in his pristine truck. "Remember the time that rescued puppy barfed in your back seat enroute to the vet? I thought you were going to throw up just telling me about it. You took it to a car wash and said, 'Just clean it up. I don't want to see it or smell it.' That was so funny to me!"

"Yeah, I am squeamish about stuff like that, and I am particular about the truck. He'll have to wait until I think of another way to transport him."

"Don't forget about the ATVs in the storage unit. You can use them when the time comes," Frau offered.

"Ok, that's what I'll have to do. I'm sure not contaminating my truck. I'll have to find something to roll him up in and put him in the bed." Now, Gino looked worried, wondering how he was going to get that smell out of his truck.

Settling in for a long night at their post with Gino pulling the first shift, Frau and Jackson got their sleeping bags ready. "There's nothing like just sitting around watching a monitor to really wear you out," Jackson remarked, shaking his sleeping bag to insure that no scorpions were hiding out.

"No kidding. The longest, most tedious days of teaching were those when we had to administer tests all day. Just watching other people work was exhausting!" Frau rolled over after checking over Gino's shoulder one last time. "Good night." She laughed. "I don't suppose Atkins' will be."

While they were secure in a shelter, Atkins was struggling with darkness and dropping temperatures. After managing to get back up to the top of the ridge, he found a rock on which to elevate his foot. He wondered for the thousandth time if it was merely sprained or fractured and whether he had exacerbated it in his mad scramble to stop his descent. *It hurts more than ever. If I don't get medical attention soon, it might be frozen. They might have to break it to set it properly*, he thought bitterly. *All because of that rhino.*

At some point, Atkins had realized that the humming sound of the drone had stopped. It had been a source of comfort for him—a lifeline to the civilization he now craved so desperately—and it was gone. He felt safer knowing that they were tracking him, that there might be hope of intervention after all.

As he lay in the dark, flicking away insects, listening to the sounds of the nocturnal animals and the call of the coyotes, he grew sleepy and eventually dozed off despite his pain.

But the respite was brief. In the distance, he heard a sound that seemed headed in his direction. Suddenly alert, he sat up and listened intently, turning his head from side to side, as if using radar to triangulate the source and distance of the sound. *Could it be?* he questioned wildly. *Is it possible?*

Not far away, three hunting enthusiasts from local ranches were riding in a helicopter piloted by a local good old boy named Bob Clark who was well-known for his night-time feral pig hunts. While it was illegal to hunt deer at night from a helicopter using spotlights, when it came to feral pigs, it was by any means necessary. They were universally loathed by the ranchers.

Occasionally, the ranchers would get liquored up and prevail on Bob to take them for a ride to "get something for the barbeque pit." While the pigs looked ferocious and ugly as hell, their meat was surprisingly tasty and tender when slow-cooked.

"I'm itchin' for some pulled pork barbeque," one of the men told Bob as he fueled the machine. Thirty minutes into the flight, they had spotted a group of feral pigs heading toward the gulley where Atkins was and were now in pursuit.

The fleeing hogs were in a blind panic, running as fast as they could to escape the noise of the helicopter and the bright lights pointing out their path.

When Atkins first heard the sound of the helicopter, he had been intrigued and sure that it was coming to rescue him, but the nearer it got to him, with the lights and what sounded like gunshots, he grew alarmed—especially since it seemed to be coming straight in his direction.

Within minutes, he could hear the grunts and squeals of the pigs in their desperate attempt to flee, along with the sound of the men's voices hollering in delight as one of them fired a shot and saw a pig stumble and come to a stop.

Oh, what fresh hell is this? The panicked Atkins thought as he tried to roll out of the way of the stampeding pigs.

The pigs never noticed that they had trampled on anything, much less a person. Some of the males weighed over three hundred pounds, and their hooves drove deep into Atkins' flesh. He screamed in agony again and again until the whole group had thundered past. He now lay motionless in a bruised and bloody heap.

When the helicopter got close enough, they almost overlooked him, so focused were they on their prey. But at the last minute, one of the men in the back said, "Hey, I think there's somebody back there. We'd better turn around and check it out!"

The pigs were long gone by the time Bob Clark landed the helicopter and the four men ran to the injured man lying motionless on the ridge.

"What the hell!" the portly rancher with the double chin and the expensive boots exclaimed as he rolled Atkins onto his back. "What's this guy doing out here all alone in the middle of nowhere at this time of night?"

Clark yelled over his shoulder as he sprinted to the helicopter for his first-aid kit, "We've got bigger things to worry about than that. We need to get him to a hospital fast before he bleeds to death!"

"Damn!" one of the men said as he leaned down to unbutton Atkins' shirt. "This guy smells like shit. It looks like he was in a losing battle with a skunk. Are we going to have to be shut up in the 'copter with this?" He looked horrified, as if the smell would permanently attach to him.

Dropping to his knees, Clark went to work, immediately wrapping bandages around the cuts and checking to see if the injured man had any broken bones.

"His left arm is broke, for sure" he declared as he used a splint and wrapped gauze tightly around it for stability. "He's lost a lot of blood, but his injuries don't seem life-threatening. But I'm no doctor. Let's put him on the stretcher and haul him to the 'copter. Oh, God, does he stink!" Clark said through clenched teeth.

The men each grabbed a corner and quickly—but gingerly—carried Atkins to the idling 'copter and loaded him into the back. He emitted a low moan as he was jostled.

"Hey, do you think we should be moving him? Maybe we should call for help," a tall rancher with a scar over his right eye said. "It might be dangerous to move him—especially if he has a neck injury."

"Well, that ship has sailed," Bob Clark countered, grunting as he tried to adjust the stretcher. "Besides, do you know how long it would take for someone to get here? This is unincorporated. I don't even know which county to call or who would respond."

As they positioned Atkins for take-off, one of the men—a rangy guy with a penchant for turquoise jewelry named Lou—said, "What are we gonna tell the authorities anyway? They're gonna want to know how and where we found this dude. They're not gonna be too happy when they find out we were out here hunting in federally protected land."

"That's why we're not going to tell them all that. We'll simply say we were hunting on my ranch. It's not that far off and the 'where' is not going to be the real issue. The 'why' is going to be what interests them."

The debate went on until they started seeing Austin's city lights and landed on the roof of the biggest hospital in the Austin area—a place where Bob Clark had landed on previous occasions. People appeared out of nowhere, rushing to remove Atkins, get his vital signs and hook him up to oxygen to stabilize him at the triage center on the roof. Once they declared him stable for transport, they rolled his gurney onto the elevator and took him to the emergency room for evaluation.

Bob Clark and his cronies followed, knowing they were going to have to answer a lot of questions.

When the feral hog stampede first began, Gino had taken no special notice of it because it was the pigs and not Atkins who were moving. But when the men in the helicopter moved Atkins for transport, Gino immediately noticed the change in location and alerted Frau and Jackson.

"Hey, Frau, something's up. All of a sudden Atkins is on the move and not at snail-pace either. He's moving way too fast considering that ankle."

Frau and Jackson popped out of their sleeping bags and raced to the monitor. Frau rubbed her eyes to get rid of her bleary-eyed blur. "Holy crap! He is moving fast! What do you think is going on?"

"Maybe a predator got him," Jackson suggested, not really believing it himself.

"I think if that happened, there'd be more random movements, like a fight where people are ducking and dodging. This is linear—like he's headed straight from Point A to Point B." Gino said, amazed by the rapid pace at which Atkins' GPS blip was moving on the screen.

"You're right," Frau said, incredulous as she watched the quick movement. "He would have fought against an attacker, even something like a mountain lion, and that would have meant some back-and-forth for sure. This is just really weird."

"Hey, maybe something took off with his backpack—you know, a coyote or something. An animal would have no idea that there is a tracking device in it. Even Atkins apparently never found it. An animal would just grab it and go." Jackson was glued to the monitor, his mind racing.

"It's possible," Gino agreed, adjusting his glasses. "But what would attract an animal to a backpack? There was no real food in it—just those energy bars. And that's virtually zero-scent to a carnivore."

"Yeah, I guess you're right. Still, if something were hungry enough . . . " Jackson trailed off.

"Okay, here's the weird thing. There were two tracking devices, right? Well, one of the devices is still at the original location where he stopped for the night, but the other one is gone—like, really gone. Look at that thing!"

They all stared at the monitor as the blips from the tracking device suddenly accelerated—coinciding with the take-off of the helicopter.

"Look at that sucker go!" Gino yelled excitedly. "It's going at warp speed and look, it's headed north back towards Austin. This whole thing is just surreal!"

"It is eerie," Jackson agreed.

"Maybe that's it." Frau said quietly.

"What?" Gino and Jackson said in unison, looking at each other like they'd been spooked.

"Maybe he got abducted by aliens," she said in a hushed voice that made the hair on the boys' necks stand on end.

17

As the Trifecta scrambled to get everything loaded into Gino's truck for the trip back to Dallas, Frau was reminding them to "use the native American approach"—leave no trace, insisting that they "even take the trash." Once everything was loaded, she went around in her obsessive/compulsive way, double-checking to insure that everything had been removed. Satisfied that all their crap was accounted for, they jumped in the truck and followed the winding road back to the highway and civilization.

"Man, I am not sad to leave that place," Jackson said as he settled into the back seat and studied his cell phone for news of the incident.

Gino wasted no time calling Juan. "Say, man, what's up?" Juan asked as he shuffled papers on his desk.

"Not much," Gino replied, deftly changing lanes to pass a slow-moving eighteen-wheeler and speeding up. "I was just wondering: Where's that limo?"

"As soon as ya'll returned it, my cousin Emilio came and got it. It's in his paint shop right now. Why?"

"I wish I could tell you. I just need for you to keep it under wraps for a while. Did he already paint it?"

"I'm not sure where they are in the process. You know it's a small shop—just him and his brother. They do a really good job custom-painting cars. They might have it for a couple of weeks," Juan replied as he spun around in his chair to grab his water and take a big gulp." You didn't get it in some kind of trouble, didja?"

"No, but the longer it's out of sight, the better. How trustworthy is Emilio? And his brother?"

Gino's tone made Juan a little nervous. "Dude, you know they're family. Do you want me to invoke the code? Because I will," Juan reassured him.

"Yeah, man, that's exactly what needs to happen. Invoke the code," Gino said, a little too eagerly. He looked in his rearview mirror for another opportunity to change lanes.

"It's done," Juan assured him. "I'll call Emilio and tell him to keep it on the down-low. No problem."

"All right, then. I'll check with you later." Gino turned to Frau. "Juan's gonna handle it."

"Great," she said. "But what's this 'code' you mentioned?" She guessed at its meaning.

"It's a code of silence, a brotherhood thing, like 'la raza unida' or something. We support each other," he explained.

"Got it. It's a Mexican thing," she said smiling. "It's a good system."

"It does come in handy." Gino accelerated to pass a red Charger.

Jackson leaned forward. "Frau, there's some information coming across the news about our boy. It looks like he's in the ICU at Austin General Hospital. He's in critical condition. He hasn't regained consciousness. The

Austin P.D. is investigating. They haven't identified him yet. They say he was found by some ranchers hunting feral hogs from a helicopter. Seems he got trampled in the chase."

"No shit!" Frau expostulated. "What the hell? He got run over by wild pigs? Oh my God! That's priceless!"

As Gino swerved slightly to avoid a road construction sign, he said, "It couldn't have happened to a more deserving guy! Well, I mean, in a way. Being trampled by pigs can't be fun, but it sure is funny!"

"No, I doubt if he's having a good time at the moment," Jackson said, sounding a little remorseful. "I mean, it kind of is our fault that he's in the mess he's in. I feel kinda bad for him." He continued scrolling, looking for updates on Atkins' condition.

"We did say 'no mercy,' you know. Maybe you should look at this as divine intervention. After all, we didn't send feral hogs after him." Frau tried to put a philosophical spin on it.

Jackson looked unconvinced. "Look, this report says the guys in the helicopter picked him up at the Winding River Ranch. That's not Mo's place, is it?"

"No, it's not. And anyway, he wasn't on Mo's property. He was in that protected area—the Balcones Fault area. What the fuck?" she glanced back to peer at his cellphone.

"That's really strange." Gino said. "Why do you suppose they would lie about where they picked him up? That helicopter accounts for why his blip on the radar accelerated so fast. They picked him up and took him to the hospital, I'm guessing."

"Obviously, they couldn't admit that they were hunting in that protected area," Jackson opined. "They'd be in a lot of trouble. That's federal land."

"True," Gino said. "They're federally protecting themselves. And that explains why they haven't identified Atkins. Remember how I showed you that one of the tracking devices took off and the other stayed behind? If they left his backpack with the tracking device behind, that's where his driver's license was, and since they couldn't admit where they really found him, no one's looking in that area. I don't know if anyone will ever find that backpack. Those hunters ' finding him may be our biggest break in this whole sorry scenario."

"No doubt about it," Frau chuckled, obviously pleased with the events. "I'm not down-playing how serious his situation is, nor am I denying the role we played, but sometimes, things just work out."

Throughout the conversation, Jackson seemed troubled. Both Frau and Gino sensed it, but neither remarked on their suspicion. Finally, Jackson said quietly, "Frau, Gino, you know this is really bothering me. I have to re-think my entire raison d'etre. This is contrary to my whole being. Fun's fun, but I'm pledged to be God's servant and look at me! I'm basically a criminal!"

Gino did not mince words. "Jackson, knock it off! You knew what you were getting into. We all did. We didn't know what was going to happen. It was out of our control. It was a survival challenge, and he succeeded, by the way. He's not dead, so that's not on your conscience. We said 'no mercy' and that's how it played out. Why do you want to beat yourself up over it? If you ask me, he got what he deserved. He's better off than The Unicorn, that's for sure."

"Okay, Gino, I see your point. It's something I'm gonna have to live with. But I think I'm gonna leave the Trifecta to you guys."

"Jackson, do what you have to do," Frau consoled him as she patted his knee. "Maybe this is a good time for you to flop."

"Oh, you know, I've been floppin' as fast as I can," Jackson replied.

'Well, if you're praying for him to recover, you know we're going to be in deep shit." Frau said as she turned in her seat to get a good look at Jackson.

"Frau, you can't mean you hope he's going to die!" Jackson looked shocked.

"Not really. It's just an observation," she said matter-of-factly. "If he regains consciousness, eventually the trail might lead to us. Just be prepared, but like I said, we really didn't do anything wrong. Maybe abandonment or something, but not criminal intent."

"I hope you're right," Jackson said, gazing out the window at the monotonous landscape.

In Austin, the news from the hospital was not promising. The mysterious stranger had still not been identified. He was still unconscious, although it was widely believed that his injuries were not life-threatening. Surgery had been performed to close some of the deep gashes left by hogs' hooves. The ranchers stood by their story because it was in their own best interest.

Austin's Chief of Police was baffled. He wasted no time assigning the case to Ray Hernandez, a veteran member of the department who had the distinction of being the youngest officer ever promoted to detective. He was renowned for solving difficult cases. That reputation stemmed from a homicide that occurred when he had been on the force for only two years.

A twenty-year-old University of Texas pre-med student named Eric Dalton had gone to Padre Island for spring break with some buddies. On the second night of their stay, he and his friends walked across the border into Mexico where they made the rounds of popular bars. At some point during the night, Eric and his friends were separated and then, he simply vanished. At first, his friends thought they would find him chatting up some girls somewhere or passed out in one of the bars they'd visited. But as night turned to day and they still had not found him, they became alarmed and alerted the authorities.

The Austin police were notified immediately and, when confronted with an investigation of international proportions, the police chief decided that the logical person to send would be bilingual. That person was Ray. There really was no choice. At the time, Ray was the senior Spanish-speaking officer, and the chief was convinced that he had the skills and gravitas to be an asset to the investigation.

Two hours later, Ray was on a flight to Mexico. At first, the locals stonewalled. He couldn't get anything out of anyone. He realized that they were scared to talk. But of what or whom?

Ray didn't relent. He visited every bar that Eric's friends recalled visiting that night. He talked to bartenders, waitresses, patrons, hookers. Many of them remembered the good-looking, blonde young gringo. But if they knew what happened to him, they weren't telling.

Ray collaborated with the Mexican police who set up roadblocks around the city and interrogated everyone leaving or entering. This was a high-profile case, and they were under tremendous pressure to solve it. After all, spring break is a major money-maker for the border towns. If people were afraid to come and spend their big bucks, the economy would suffer.

Ray was persistent. Eventually, one of the waitresses—a young woman who attended college on the American side of the border—gave Ray the break that he needed. She recalled serving the "cute" American. He had been nice to her and tipped generously. She wanted to help find him. The waitress made Ray swear that he would not implicate her, and then she gave him the name of a rancho ten miles away.

The Mexican police knew the place well. It belonged to a powerful family whose fortune stemmed from smuggling drugs. They were universally feared by the townspeople. Their evil deeds were notorious.

When Ray and the police arrived at the ranch, they headed to some ramshackle outbuildings far removed from the main house. As they surveyed the scene, it wasn't immediately clear what they had discovered. Animal parts, feathers, candles, black pots and incense were scattered in the second shed they entered. Ray looked puzzled, but the situation quickly became obvious. Ray made the unfortunate discovery of a human skull in one of the pots. All hell broke loose. The ranch was flooded with police, which attracted the media, and the story quickly went global.

Ray was in the center of it all. When DNA confirmed that the skull was indeed Eric's, Ray helped make the arrests. He also supervised the excavation—conducted by the murder suspects—of a burial ground that yielded fifteen bodies in various stages of decay. The scene was horrific. The murderers gagged and puked and cried and begged to be relieved. But they were shown no mercy. It was Mexican justice. The stench was overwhelming. Ray never flinched. He persevered throughout the ordeal, collecting evidence from the graves and labeling body parts that he placed in plastic bags.

In the aftermath, he talked to the boy's parents, endeavoring to be as tactful and sensitive as possible. Because what their son had suffered was so unbelievable in the modern age—so completely medieval, so utterly contemptible—that he left the crime scene in tears every day. How could he explain such evil to Christian people? There was no explanation, just gory facts and details. He anguished over how to spare them the gruesome end of their precious son's life. But he realized he couldn't.

In the end, Eric's parents thanked him for his professionalism and courtesy, as well as his commitment to following the investigation through to its disgusting conclusion. Every year thereafter, Ray received a Christmas card from the Dalton family. It cemented his resolve to be a consummate investigator.

Consequently, when the police chief called Ray in, the office was already rife with rumors that he would be assigned the case of the swine-stomped stranger.

"What's up, Chief?" Ray asked nonchalantly. Although he already had an inkling, he decided to play along.

"Ray, you've no doubt heard about the guy that Bob Clark and his buddies ran across in one of their evening forays. The guy that's over in ICU at Austin General?"

"Yeah, I've got the gist of it." Ray downplayed his knowledge of the case. He had already been briefed by one of the chief's subordinates.

"I'd like for you to take it on," the chief said, looking at Ray for traces of disinterest or apathy.

"You know I've got a lot going on right now," Ray replied, knowing that he would indeed accept the assignment. He enjoyed toying with the chief. It was one of the perks of an otherwise mundane job.

"Come on, Ray. You and I both know you're cut out for this one. You like challenges, and this one is earmarked for your detective skills. Consider it a personal favor. I didn't even consider anyone else." The chief looked tired. "It's become a big deal."

"How so?" Ray looked genuinely puzzled. He thought it was just a run-of-the-mill case.

"The media boys are having a little too much fun with it. Theories are springing up. There's a lot of speculation about who he is and how he came to be trampled by the hogs. Our reputation is taking a beating."

"Yeah, I've seen some of the cartoons and heard the jokes: 'pickled in pig's feet'; 'the swine strike back'; 'don't mess with hogs in Texas'; 'Texas gives a new twist to hog heaven.' It's brutal," he said chuckling quietly.

"Okay, it's funny, but this guy is lying critically injured in our regional hospital, and we don't know who he is so we can notify his family."

"All right, Chief. Just for you. I'll go on over to the hospital and check on him. Shall I give him your regards?"

"Do whatever you want. Just find out who he is, so we can get him out of here. His family must be missing him." The chief looked amused but weary. The mayor was putting pressure on him to solve the case and put a positive spin on it. He was already tired of being the butt of jokes: "The Mayor of Pork City." The popular expression "Keep Austin weird" was turning into "How weird can Austin get?"

After his meeting with the chief, Ray headed over to Austin General to check on the stranger's condition. The ICU nurse told him there had been no change. The patient was still unconscious but his vital signs were stable, and he was expected to make a full recovery. No one had contacted the hospital looking for him.

Ray went into the man's room to look him over. His face was badly battered and swollen beyond recognition. He had lacerations on his arms and stitches in several areas of his body. "Dude," Ray said softly. "I need to know who you are so I can find out if we even have a case." To the nurse, he said, "Notify me if there's any change or if anyone comes looking for him."

Two days later, Ray got a call. "No change in the patient's condition," the nurse told him. "But someone claiming to be his wife called the hospital looking for him." She gave Ray the caller's number.

Ray contacted Marissa Atkins immediately. She told him that her husband Jeff Atkins had left home on Friday, saying that he was going "hunting with the boys." When he didn't return or call, and someone told her the story of the man who had been injured by pigs during a hunt on a Texas ranch, she grew concerned and started making inquiries. It didn't sound like Jeff's modus operandi. His usual hunting spots were far from Texas, but she was clearly concerned that it might be her husband. She agreed to fly to Austin as soon as she could get a flight.

As soon as he heard the man's name, Ray made the connection: "Oh, yeah, the rhino-killer."

Ray picked up Mrs. Atkins at the airport. *Not a bad-looking woman*, he thought. On the way to the hospital, she asked him over and over about the condition of the man she presumed was her husband. When told the story, she snorted in disbelief. "That can't be my husband. He wouldn't be caught dead hunting feral hogs. That's beneath him."

Ray declined to point out the obvious—that he wasn't hunting hogs. He had been ravaged by hogs that were being hunted by guys in a helicopter. Not a fine distinction, but a valid point. He resented her snobby dismissal of hunting in Texas.

Upon arrival at the hospital, Ray ushered Mrs. Atkins to the third floor ICU to see if she could positively identify the battered man. When she saw him, lying in the hospital bed with oxygen tubes, i.v. lines and bloody stitches, she moaned, "Oh, my God. Poor Jeff. Poor baby. How did this happen?"

Ray gave her time to process the situation. When she calmed down, he asked her: "Did your husband tell you anything about this trip? Who he was joining? Where he was staying? How long he'd be gone?"

"No, "she replied softly. "Jeff and I had an understanding. He didn't ask me about my vacations with my friends, and I didn't ask him about his hunting expeditions. We pretty much went our separate ways. The less we knew about our individual activities, the better we liked it." She blew her nose and wiped her eyes as she spoke.

He wrote rapidly in a little notebook. "Well, this time, it didn't work to his advantage," Ray remarked wryly as he snapped his notebook shut.

"Is there any chance he'll regain consciousness? This is already day three, isn't it?" she asked as she leaned forward, brushing Atkins' hair out of his face.

"According to the doctor that I talked to," Ray began, "It's all in God's hands. If you believe in that sort of thing.

They can't rush the recovery process. All they can do is offer medical support until the swelling in his brain subsides. He took a beating. It could be days or weeks or . . ." He trailed off.

"It may never happen. Is that what you're telling me? Oh, my God. Jeff! Jeff! Wake up now! It's Marissa!" Her anguish was palpable.

"Keep talking to him, "Ray advised. "I'm told that hearing is the last sense to shut down. Maybe hearing a familiar voice will stir something in his memory. Anyway, it can't hurt." Ray slipped out to call the police chief with the news. "We have a positive i.d.," he said. "It's Jeff Atkins. His wife confirmed it. She's with him now."

"The rhino guy? You've got to be fuckin' kidding me! This just gets worse and worse! A professional killer like that gets his ass kicked in Austin by wild hogs? That's just great!" He hung up the phone in exasperation and yelled at his assistant, "Get me that reporter on the line—the guy that's covering the pig incident. I've got news!"

18

After the news was released, there was an initial flurry of activity from reporters across the globe, but as the days passed and there was no change in his condition, the reporters gradually lost interest. Marissa Atkins played the role of devoted wife, keeping vigil at her husband's hospital bed as he struggled to recover from his injuries. After five days, his eyelids began to flutter when she spoke to him, and a day or two later, he weakly squeezed her fingers in recognition. Two weeks after he was admitted, he began trying to speak, but his speech was so labored and garbled, it was virtually unintelligible. Eventually, his wife reported to Ray that Atkins had made utterances that sounded like "Black Momma," "Cobra," and "Viper," but she dismissed those as rantings borne of her husband's snake-phobia. Not long after that, Atkins was transported to a rehab facility for physical and speech therapy.

Despite his best efforts, Ray was unable to surmount the obstacles that lay in his path to solving the case. Every day, he went dutifully to the hospital—and later, the rehab facility—to check on Atkins' progress. Then he would make the rounds of the four ranchers' homes to question them further about their involvement, but they never wavered from their original story. None of the employees at the airport recalled seeing Atkins, and security videos were inconclusive. There was one video showing someone who could have been Atkins getting into a camouflage-painted limousine, but Ray had not been able to ferret out such a limo in the Austin area. It seemed that every avenue he pursued was a dead-end. Finally, he had to admit to his chief that he had made no headway in solving Atkins' case. Even after two weeks in rehab, Atkins' memory and speech were still impaired. Most of his long-term memory returned, but he had no recollection of coming to Austin, how he got there, or whom he was with. It had all been inconveniently erased and, unless it did come back, the case was, for all practical purposes, closed.

Mrs. Atkins prepared her husband for the trip home six weeks after the widely-heralded "feral hog attack," hoping that she would never again have to set foot in Texas.

In Dallas, the Trifecta had to be content with monitoring media reports about the case and updates on Atkins' condition. They knew if they made any inquiries, they would be opening themselves up for investigation. Biding their time was difficult. When it was reported that Atkins had made progress and was gradually regaining his memory, they held their collective breath.

Not long after Atkins' identity was made public, Frau received a call from MoMo. "How ya doin', Frau?" he asked nonchalantly.

"MoMo!" Frau was delighted to hear from him. "What's going on with you, Big Guy?"

"Oh, nothing much. Just wanted to check on you to see how you enjoyed your weekend in Austin," he remarked disingenuously. "I hope everything was to your liking." She could hear the smile in his voice.

"It was just great," she lied. "We had a nice little getaway. It's always good to escape from the noise and confusion of the city." She wondered if he had a hidden agenda or if he was genuinely interested in her visit. "I do hope we left your property in good shape."

"I never would have known you'd been here except for Hank. He told me he escorted you in, but that was it. He never heard anything from you. He didn't even know when you'd left. When he went to check on you, there wasn't even a trace that you'd been there," he hinted.

"That's exactly the way I like it," she responded. "I'm a little Native American on my mother's side, and I value the environment. I try to leave it pristine whenever I camp anywhere," she assured him.

"Well, good job," he laughed. "Just so you know, there was a little trouble on a neighboring ranch. My old buddy, Bob Clark, had a little adventure when he was hunting wild hogs. It seems he ran across a guy who was trespassing on his property, but the hogs got to him first. It was a little messy, but, apparently, all is well."

"Do tell," she said, a little nervously.

"Yeah, he's a good old boy, kind of a heavy hitter down here. He's politically connected, owns a lot of property. He's highly respected, always supports me in my political endeavors. He plays his cards close to the chest. I can always depend on him to be loyal to the cause, and his friends are loyal to him. I'm glad things worked out because I wouldn't want anything to compromise his integrity. The authorities have cleared him completely of any complicity in the matter." MoMo sounded relieved. "It's actually a good thing for the trespasser that Bob came along when he did. Otherwise, that idiot might have been fodder for the coyotes."

"I'm glad everything worked out for the best. Thanks for your hospitality. If I can do anything to return the favor, be sure and let me know," she offered sincerely.

"My official campaign start date is June 1st. I hope I can count on you to help me out in Dallas. You seem to know a lot of people, especially on the south side, and that's where I need a boost," he said.

"You got it, MoMo. I'm there for you. I can make calls, set up events, whatever you need. I told you before, I owe you big-time!" She chuckled as she hung up. *He can sure be diplomatic*, she thought. *Without saying anything, he got his point across.*

Soon after, Frau put in a call to Pam to see if she'd been following the story.

"What's up, Miss Pam?" she asked cheerfully.

"Ain't nuttin', Baby Girl. What's up with you? I heard about your little excitement down in Austin." Pam chuckled mischievously. "I hear you got our boy good."

"Well," Frau replied. "I don't know if that's exactly true. It seems that some feral hogs did my job for me. It was quite unexpected, but somehow, it seems like divine intervention. Anyway, I don't think he'll be doing any big game hunting any time soon. That's the real story." She laughed. "I really wish you had been there. You would have enjoyed the trip."

"I know. I'm just glad that everything worked out and you guys got back safe. I was a little concerned that something would go wrong, and I'd have to come bail you out. You know I'd do it!" Pam assured her.

"I know. That's why I love you," Frau responded sincerely.

"Oh, by the way. The Pussy Parlor will be open Thursday. I'm bringing my cat Vinnie in to shave him down. You're welcome to bring your matted pussies to the clinic. I'll shave their hairy asses down to the bone!" Pam had a lovely way with words that Frau admired.

"You bet I'll be there! They are definitely looking ragged. I look forward to seeing you then!" Frau shook her head as she hung up the phone.

After his initial misgiving, Jackson came to terms with his part in the Atkins escapade. When they first returned to Dallas, he had distanced himself from the Trifecta for a while. But he soon realized that he had enjoyed the adrenaline rush of what he called "their little adventure."

"Frau," he told her on the phone one afternoon, "I'm actually craving a little excitement. Things are so dull right now."

"Don't worry, Jackson," she assured him. "It won't be long before we mount a new campaign. Just yesterday, there was a news report about an asshole who got liquored up on St. Patrick's Day, went home and tortured and killed his little dog. He needs to go down! I want to drown him in a vat of green beer." Jackson could hear her sniffling a little. Although she attributed it to allergies, he knew better.

"Please let me do it, Frau," he said. "I saw that on the news, too, and I had the same reaction. People like that are no good to anyone. The sooner he's put out of commission, the better." He absent-mindedly picked up a cross from his desk and gave it a quick spin. "That guy is right here in town."

"True, but he's still in jail at the moment. There's too much scrutiny on him right now. We need to wait for the clamor to die down, but don't worry. Justice will be served." She sounded determined.

"No doubt about it," Jackson agreed. "When are we going to get together again?"

"We'll have to get together soon for burgers and beer. The weather's been perfect for a grillfest. We can strategize then."

"Sounds good," he said, "Just let me know." He hung up and returned the cross to its upright position.

19

A month later, unknown to Gino and Jackson, Frau was in Canada, preparing to embark on an all-out assault on the fur industry's hired seal-killers. Her trip was the culmination of three years of networking and covert planning. She knew Gino and Jackson would be angry that she didn't include them, but she felt strongly that this was a project she would have to undertake alone. There was too much risk, for one thing. And for another, it was such a clandestine operation, she didn't want to compromise her own involvement by trying to get them included. She had been working with an undercover animal advocacy group to pull off this wide-scale offensive. She couldn't wait to get started. It had been a dream of hers for some time to take a stand against the heinous criminals who club the little baby seals and skin them alive, leaving them to die a slow, excruciating death on the ice. It was horrific and unconscionable. If this was to be her swan song, she would go out happy.

Frau had waited a long time for this opportunity and was elated that it was finally about to happen. Months before, she had volunteered for "interference duty," which meant she was to insert herself between the baby seals and their killers. By law, the interference team could only use spray paint on the seals to render their furs useless for commercial purposes. They could also harass the killers, making it difficult for them to get to the seals. But being a bit of a rogue, and figuring that this was probably her one shot, Frau had another tool up her sleeve—a concealed club that she intended to use with deadly force, if necessary. She was all-in.

As the Champion of the Seas bobbed off-shore with men using loudspeakers, continually yelling at the killer squad to "cease and desist their crimes against nature," the launches carrying the volunteers were racing to the icy home of the seals.

The mother seals were crammed together with their newborns in their snow-white furs as they shyly snuggled close for warmth and protection. The Champion volunteers landed moments before the official start time of the killing season, just in time to face their formidable foes. The killers wore ski masks, more to disguise their identities than to protect themselves from the cold, because they feared being targeted by vigilante groups during the off-season. Their face-less facades gave them an even more sinister appearance, spurring the volunteers to re-double their commitment to win this fight against evil.

Frau wasted no time disembarking from the launch. With a fierce cry, she zeroed in on one of the killers who was already using an airhorn to frighten a mother seal away from her helpless pup so he could skin it alive. Frau took the offense, running at him and screaming like a banshee from hell as she attacked him from behind, clambering onto his back and grabbing him around the throat. He flung her to the ground and quickly advanced toward the terrified baby seal. Frau rolled over, spray can in hand, and managed to shoot two rounds of green paint on the baby.

Angry, the killer turned on her and said, "You're going to regret getting involved in this. Back off!" He advanced on her in a threatening manner, then turned toward another target.

This time, she wasted no energy. She grabbed her hidden club and slammed it as hard as she could across his back. When he yelled in pain and struggled to regain his footing, she kicked him with steel-toed boots in the stomach. As he fell to the ground, she raised her club as high over her head as she could and brought it down on his knees again and again, shattering them both and leaving him quivering and helpless on the ice.

"No mercy!" she screamed at him savagely. The look in her eyes was primitive and animalistic. "I hope you die, you miserable bastard! While you're lying there, unable to move, remember, I could kill you right now if I wanted to. Just ask yourself: Is it worth it? Whatever the fur company is paying you, is it worth your life?" She glared at him menacingly before taking off after another killer nearby.

Although the volunteers had been given strict instructions and warned repeatedly that infractions would be penalized by law, it was difficult to regulate what happened in the actual throes of battle. Afterward, people reported that one of the volunteers had "gone berserk" and was just battering members of the killer squad, but no one tried to stop her and no one could identify the actual culprit. Since everyone was dressed in a <u>Champion of the Seas</u> thermal suit, there were no distinguishing characteristics. In the heat of the campaign, details of size, weight and gender were inconsequential. It was said the rogue volunteer was like winged fury, flying from one killer to another, knocking them down and beating them senseless as baby seals scampered to the safety of their mothers. Much of the blood on the ice belonged to her victims, rather than the seals.

During her rampage, Frau was oblivious to everything around her. She was in the zone –a wrecking machine programmed for revenge. All of her senses shut down. She operated on pure anger and adrenaline. She went from point to point, spray-painting baby seals whenever she could and incapacitating their killers with strategic strikes to elbows and knees. She was focused on her objective and relentless in her pursuit. Although she knew she couldn't save them all, her single-minded goal was to stop as many killers as possible, at any cost. Pounding in her head was the staccato opening to "O Fortuna!" from the opera Carmina Burana, the perfect backdrop for her rampage.

The assault on the baby seal- killers made international news, and the mystery volunteer was universally applauded for his/her triumph over the criminal fur industry. The Canadian government threatened legal action.

For her part, Frau awoke the next day, exhausted and aching, but blissful. Every bone in her body screamed for relief, but no one could erase the smile on her face. She had achieved a goal—the imperfect fulfillment of a dream—and she was at peace for the first time in many, many years.

20

She rolled over in her bed to reach for her cellphone and made a conference call to Gino and Jackson. "You won't believe where I am and what I've been doing," she told them, laughing.

"Frau, whatever it is, I can hear the smile on your face over the phone," Gino said, surprised at how carefree she sounded.

"Yeah, Frau, you sound like you just won the lottery," Jackson added, wondering what could have possibly put her in such a jovial mood.

"Well, boys, you might have guessed, if you keep up with the news. I'm in Canada. Baby seal season started yesterday, and I got to participate in the campaign against the fur industry's slaughter. I am so happy, I can't even explain it! Ow, Ow," she cried in pain as she reached down for her slippers. "This has opened my eyes to what we can do on an even bigger scale. I feel unstoppable. There's nothing we can't accomplish!" She winced in pain as she sat up and tried to get out of bed. "I'm a little achy right now, but I'll get over it. A little Icy Hot, and I'm as good as new." She laughed as she stretched to work out the stiffness. "I'm good to go another round. So whaddya think? Elephants? Snow leopards? I'm on a roll. You decide. I'm thinking Africa would be lovely this time of year."

"Frau," they said in unison. "Your call. Let's go."

"I'll research Orbitz right now. By the time you get back, I'll have everything arranged," Gino promised.

"All right, boys. See you Saturday at my place. Burgers and beer. And an African adventure. I can't wait," she said, ending the call on an elated note. "Let's do this!"

Cynthia Herschkowitsch

Cynthia Herschkowitsch, a resident of Carrollton, Texas, taught English and German in Dallas, Texas, for 39 years. In 1987-88, she was named Dallas Independent School District's Teacher of the Year. During her career, she coached Academic Decathlon, served as coordinator for graduation activities, and coordinated the University Interscholastic League academic events. For over 20 years, she hosted a Christmas party for needy children at the school with the help of her students and was twice named Fox 4's "Hometown Hero" by news anchor Clarice Tinsley for her charitable work. She is a regular contributor to the Neighborhood Voices column of the Dallas Morning News and remains active in education and community activities. She has also been an animal rescuer for 30 years, working closely with the SPCA of Texas in Dallas, Operation Kindness, and Stray Dog, Inc. Her favorite pastimes are traveling, reading, and spending time with family, friends and pets, especially her little dog, J.B. She especially enjoys collaborating with her daughter Delia and her former students on special events.

Made in the USA
Monee, IL
08 June 2020